The BILL WALLACE Collection

THE MEANEST HOUND AROUND

THE BACKWARD BIRD DOG

WATCHDOG AND THE COYOTES

The BILL WALLACE Collection

THE MEANEST HOUND AROUND

THE BACKWARD BIRD DOG

WATCHDOG AND THE COYOTES

ALADDIN PAPERBACKS
NEW YORK LONDON TORONTO SYDNEY

This book is a work of fiction. Any references to historical events, real people, or real locales are used fictitiously. Other names, characters, places, and incidents are the product of the author's imagination, and any resemblance to actual events or locales or persons, living or dead, is entirely coincidental.

ALADDIN PAPERBACKS
An imprint of Simon & Schuster Children's Publishing Division
1230 Avenue of the Americas, New York, NY 10020

The Meanest Hound Around
Text copyright © 2003 by Carol Wallace and Bill Wallace
Illustrations copyright © 2003 by John Steven Gurney

The Backward Bird Dog
Text copyright © 1997 by Bill Wallace
Illustrations copyright © 1997 by David Slonim

Watchdog and the Coyotes
Text copyright © 1995 by Bill Wallace
Illustrations copyright © 1995 by David Slonim

Manufactured in the United States of America
First Aladdin Paperbacks bindup edition May 2007
ISBN-13: 978-1-4169-5100-1
ISBN-10: 1-4169-5100-8

The BILL WALLACE Collection

THE MEANEST HOUND AROUND

BY CAROL WALLACE AND BILL WALLACE

ILLUSTRATED BY JOHN STEVEN GURNEY

To
Marian Staton
and
Jennifer Brock

CHAPTER 1

Wet. I never felt so wet. I was soaked. Trying to make myself smaller, I hunched my shoulders and leaned to the right. A rivulet of water streamed down from the big limb above my head. The drops hit smack-dab between my shoulder blades.

Leaning to the left, I got away from that stream, but more water leaked from a knot on the other side of the limb. It hit right between my ears, trickled down to the tip of my snout, and dripped off my whiskers.

Beneath this huge tree was the driest spot I had found. Even so, I was still drenched—soaked clear to the skin. Water even dripped from my tummy, adding to the puddle at my feet.

I couldn't understand. My boy would never leave me out here . . . not all night . . . not all alone. . . .

We played chase in the backyard. He petted me and hugged me. I licked his face and ears and he laughed. I loved him. He loved me. My boy would never desert me.

Just then a big drop of rain hit right inside my ear. I flinched and shook my head.

It wasn't my boy. It was the daddy. He was the one who brought me here.

The day had started out okay. My boy fed me, petted me, and we'd had a little romp. When my boy left for school, the daddy put me on my leash and we went for a drive in the car. I should have known then, because there was something different about the way he acted. Something strange and unusual. Besides that, my boy wasn't with us. He was always there when we went for a ride.

I sat in the backseat and watched the road. Things didn't look familiar when we stopped. The daddy took my collar off and let me run. But when I came back to the car . . . the car was gone. Maybe I romped and played too long. Maybe I didn't come back when I should have. I don't know.

Anyway, I sat and waited and waited and waited. I just knew he wouldn't leave me.

The first night was really bad. When I was little I'd slept in a big basket with my mother and brothers and sisters. When my boy took me to live with him, I had to sleep outside. I had my own doghouse, though, and there was a big fence to keep all the nighttime scaries from getting too close. Out here, I was all alone with no place to hide. Then it got worse. It started to rain. Two days and one night the rain fell. Still I waited. I just knew they would come for me. Cold, miserable, scared, and lonely, I waited. Now . . . I'd waited long enough. It was time to move on.

Someone growled at me. It snapped me from my thoughts and made me jump. The growl came again, but this time I realized that it wasn't someone growling at me . . . it was my tummy.

3

With a heavy heart (not to mention my heavy wet fur) I knew it was time to go. I couldn't wait any longer.

As I walked I looked for anything familiar. When the rain finally stopped, I didn't. I kept walking. Never slowing down, I sniffed for those special scents of home. They weren't there.

What I did smell was kind of interesting, though. It was like the car and the trash and metal and . . . well, it reeked of everything all jumbled together. I followed the aroma to a big chain-link fence. It was like the one in my backyard, only taller. The top had wire wrapped around it. I had never seen anything quite like it. There was stuff piled everywhere. My nose wiggled as I whiffed along the edge of the fence. With all that junk and trash, there had to be *something* in there to eat.

"Get away from here, you mangy mutt!" a short black dog snarled at me. "This is my yard. Get on your way. I have work to do."

"Chill, mister, I'm just looking. Besides I don't know how to get in there anyway." I stared at the white teeth that shined back at me.

4

"I'm serious. You'd better get away from here. I mean it!" The dog's ears flattened against his head and his eyes narrowed. At the same time, though, his tail was wagging. He stuck his nose through one of the chain-link squares.

My tail started wagging, too. I leaned down and licked his nose with my pink tongue.

"Hey, stop that!" His light brown eyebrows crooked as he stepped back and growled again. The fur on his neck stood out to make him look bigger.

I dropped my head to stare him in the eye. "You need to calm down. You're going to wear out the fur on your neck."

"Get real! If I let you hang around, the junk-yard guy will kick me. I've got work to do." The dog stepped back up to the fence and sniffed at me.

I licked his face again. "Hey, what's your name, anyway?" I asked.

"Which name do you want?"

"You have more than one name? How did that happen?"

"Well, these guys call me Spike. But my first name was April."

My nose twitched and my ears perked up. "April? That's a funny name for a *boy* dog."

"Yeah, maybe, but I kind of like it. This little kid gave me that name. She was pretty sweet to me. She was a bit rough, I guess, but nothing compared to Roy. He is just mean!" The dog sat down on his haunches and relaxed.

"What should I call you?" I twitched my ears at him.

"Better call me Spike. If Tiger hears anyone call me April, I'll be in more trouble than ever." He stretched out, crossed his front legs, then dropped his head to rest on his paws.

"Who's Tiger?" I asked.

"Tiger is the Junkyard Dog. He is *really* mean. Roy has been poking him with a stick and kicking him forever. So he got his attitude adjusted a long time ago. Roy is working on me, but I'm not mean yet. He says that I'll get there, though." Spike scooted on the ground until his nose touched the fence. "By the way, what's your name?"

"Freddie. Call me Freddie." I closed my eyes. . . .

* * *

The boy had picked me special. I was the third one to leave the litter. He had looked me all over and declared, "You are Fred D. Fluff Dog! I will love you forever."

That was before the car ride. The ride that got me here . . . the junkyard. . . .

"Just call me Freddie." I sighed. "That's what my friends call me. Just Freddie." My ears drooped. My stomach grumbled.

From the back of the yard a big yellow dog came running at us.

"Spike, what are you doing? Run that white pile of fluff away from here. You aren't doing your job. Get busy! Get rid of that mutt!" I could see the dog's huge muscles under his short golden hair. Black stripes stretched across his chest and back.

Spike sprang to his feet and spun to face him. "I . . . er, I . . . ah . . . thought that was only people that we had to keep away," he stammered. "This is just a dog!"

My new friend looked sort of small and helpless as he stood next to the other dog.

"What are you thinking? One more dog

8

around here, and we won't get anything to eat. We barely get enough as it is. Get rid of him. Now!" Tiger snapped his strong jaws at Spike's ear.

"Get out of here, you big fluff ball," Spike growled at me. Then he winked. "Go around the corner and wait," he whispered softly so Tiger couldn't hear.

I looked into his narrowed eyes, flipped my tail, and ran out of sight. Hiding behind some wooden boxes, I waited for some kind of signal. It wasn't long before I heard a friendly yip.

Carefully peeking around the edge of the boxes, I kept my ears low in case Tiger was still there. Spike stood next to the fence.

"It's okay," he said with a wag of his tail. "Tiger has gone on patrol. I'm supposed to keep you away. Just make sure that you watch out for him. It takes quite awhile for Tiger to get all the way around the whole yard. What are you doing here, anyway? You look like somebody has been taking care of you." Spike stretched out and touched his nose against the fence.

I shrugged my ears. "I got dumped. I think."

Spike arched an eyebrow. "What happened?"

"I don't know. I thought the daddy was taking me for a car ride. I got out for a run, and when I came back . . ." My head drooped when I thought about it.

"Yeah, you got dumped, all right! It happens to the best of us. Things are going along just dandy, and the next thing you know . . . dumped!" Spike jumped up and started biting at his rear end. "Pesky fleas!"

"I didn't do anything. My boy and I were happy together. He loved me. I am sure of it." My heart raced as I remembered the feeling I had when the car didn't come back for me.

"You didn't *have* to do anything! Stuff just happens. Something went wrong with them. Your boy probably still loves you. It's his parents with the problem. Who knows. You gotta live for the day." Spike reached up to scratch his belly with his hind leg.

"I don't know." I sighed. "Maybe if I had minded them better. I got along great with my boy. Maybe I dug too many holes in the yard. Maybe I barked too much." I sagged to the ground and rested my nose against the fence.

"Yeah, maybe, but quit worrying about it. People are just like that. Sometimes there's no reason at all. *You can't trust people.* At least you are free. Look at the mess I'm in. You are the first dog that I have had a chance to talk to. Tiger won't even play chase with me. Well, he does, but he bites me if he catches me—really hard. If you think you have it bad, you need to be in my yard for a while."

"How could it be worse?" I sighed. "One day I have a warm house in a nice safe yard. A boy and toys to play with. Then . . . I get dumped."

Spike gave a snort. It was so loud it almost sounded like a growl. "You think you got it bad? Well, just let me tell you about bad. . . ."

CHAPTER 2

"My life started out pretty good, I guess."
Spike's ears perked up when he glanced over
his shoulder. "Be sure you watch out for Tiger
behind me."

"Okay." I nodded.

"My ma was super," he went on. "I only had
two sisters and two brothers, so we had lots of
time to play and plenty to eat. It was great. My
first home was a really nice doghouse. It was
close to the people. They watched us and kept
us safe from coyotes and dangerous stuff out in
the woods. There were two little kids there.
They played with us all the time. They even
took us for walks. When we got tired, one of

them would pick us up and snuggle up close." Spike stretched out on his belly with his front paws crossed.

"How did you end up here?" I asked.

"That's a good question. We dug in the yard, we chased butterflies, we barked at cars that came up to the house. Things were great. Our people started giving us dog food, mixed with milk. One day Ma started getting cranky with us. She snarled at us when we got too close to her. I don't know what happened." Spike snapped his head around and chewed at his side.

"I think she was trying to wean you. It was time for you to be on your own." I flopped down on my stomach, still keeping my nose against the fence.

"Yeah, I guess. Anyhow it wasn't long before Roy came to the house and picked up my sister Joy and me. I don't know what happened to her. I fell asleep in the car. When I woke up, I was stuck in a little cage. Roy kept me there for a long time. He barely fed me and he didn't keep my cage clean. It was awful." Spike jumped up, chased his tail, then tumbled onto his back and rolled in the rocks. He started chewing at the fleas again.

"That doesn't sound too good, but at least you didn't get dumped!" I stood up and shook my fur. Watching Spike bite at his fleas made me itch all over.

"Hang on, it gets worse. While I was stuck in the little cage, Tiger would come by and growl and snap at me. Ma was cranky, but nothing compared to Tiger. Every time he patrolled the yard, he made sure that he stuck his big ugly face up to my cage. Then there was Roy."

"What did Roy do?"

"At first he just stuck a stick in the cage and jabbed me. I pushed myself as far from him as possible, but I just couldn't get away. I didn't growl or bark or anything. So he got some kind of thing that stung me. I started snarling when that happened. Roy would laugh and do it again. It was terrible. He didn't let me out of that little cage until I was almost too big for it." Spike suddenly jumped to all four feet. He perked his ears and looked all around.

"Did you hear Tiger?"

He shook his head. "Guess it was just my imagination."

"Was it better after you got out of the cage?" I stared at him.

"Sort of." He stopped again and tilted his head to one side. "Do you hear anything? We don't want Tiger or Roy to catch us."

I sat up and perked my ears. "I don't hear a sound."

"Yeah, things did get a little bit better. I could hide sometimes, but mostly I had to be on patrol. If Roy caught me asleep, he'd poke me with the sting stick. If I growled, he left me alone. If not, I got jabbed again. It's been like that for a long time." Spike shook the dust off.

"Well, he feeds you, doesn't he? I haven't eaten in two days. Do you have anything that you can share with me?"

"Yeah, he feeds us. He even has our bowls in different places so that Tiger can't get all my food. It's almost time to eat, I think. Follow me. I'll show you where my bowl is. I'll share some with you. Come on." Spike trotted away from the fence and disappeared behind some car parts.

I squinted my eyes to see where he went. There were piles of junk on the outside of the fence, as well as on the inside. Moving around the clutter, I kept watch. Tiger didn't scare me, 'cause I was outside the fence. But I didn't want Spike to get in trouble. Roy was something else. If nice people dumped good dogs like me, and Roy poked sweet dogs like Spike with a sting stick . . . I had to be careful.

I strolled behind a stack of wood, then around some old metal barrels. When I got back to the fence I could see Spike's doghouse on the other side. It was wood with cracks between the boards where cold rain and wind could whistle through. His empty bowl leaned against his house.

"It won't be too long before Roy or Zack brings some food." Spike flipped his head around. "You'll have to hide when they come up."

"Who's Zack?"

"Zack works here sometimes. He isn't mean like Roy, but he has to act like he is or Roy gets mad." Spike shoved a toenail of his hind foot into his ear and scratched another flea.

"What time do they feed you? I'm starving."

"I think I hear him now. You've got to hide.

Go back by those bushes until he leaves."

As soon as I started off, Spike hopped to his feet. Tail wagging, he spun around to go greet a short, skinny man with a bald head.

As soon as I got to the bushes, I flattened out and tried to hide in the dirt.

"Hey, Spike! How's it going?" When the man smiled his greeting, he looked kind of funny. All his teeth were crooked and there was a big, black, empty space where one of his front teeth should have been. Still, he seemed nice. "You doing your job today?" the man asked as he poured dry dog food into Spike's bowl. Cautious . . . almost nervous, he glanced all around as if to make sure no one was watching. Then he dropped down and rubbed Spike's ears. "Gotta go! Be a mean dog."

I lay perfectly still until the man was gone.

"Hey, Freddie. Come and get it!" Spike shoved the bowl with his nose until it was almost to the fence.

Taking one last look all around, I raced to him.

"Sorry." He sighed. "But this is the best I can do." Quick as he could, Spike began shoveling dog food through the fence with his snout.

I ate a few of the pieces. They were hard, but just the sound of food crunching made my tummy feel better. Spike nibbled at his meal.

Suddenly his ears shot up, and he jerked his head around.

"Look out! Here comes Tiger!"

I spun and ran for some barrels.

"Grrr—get out of here you mangy dog! I've already warned you to stay away." Spike growled low in his throat.

"Did you let that dirty ball of fur come back here?" Tiger snarled at Spike, then jumped at the fence with his front paws. His lips curled back and his teeth looked wet and shiny.

I ducked behind one of the barrels, waited a second, then peeked around it. Tiger was snarling and biting at Spike.

"You trying to get us in trouble? Don't let that shabby canine near here. Roy's coming and he's going to be mad. You know better than to let some strange dog near the place."

Tiger towered over Spike. All I could do was watch as he snapped and growled at my new friend.

"What are you two filthy beasts doing out here?" Suddenly another man was standing over the dogs kicking at both of them. He poked them with a tree branch.

"Grrr . . . Leave me alone!" Tiger stood tall and straight as he growled back.

"Shut up, you nasty scoundrel. I'm in charge here." Roy kicked him in the side.

Tiger let out a little yelp and backed away. Spike ran to hide behind a pile of wood. I flattened myself against the ground as I watched the scene in front of me.

The man chased after Tiger and grabbed him by the neck, shoving him to the ground. The vicious dog snarled and growled, but he didn't bite the man.

"Shut up before I throw your ugly tail in a cage. You're supposed to be keeping robbers out of my junkyard, not fighting with the other dog. Go on, get!" Roy turned and stomped away.

Tiger started licking his side where the man had kicked him. Spike's head hung low as he cowered back toward his bowl to finish his meal. For no reason and with no warning, Tiger tore into him.

Teeth bared, he slashed and snapped at the smaller dog. Spike fell to the ground and tried to protect his throat.

"This is all your fault. Keep that dog away from here. If I catch you being nice to him again, I'll chew you up for good." Tiger swaggered away.

Spike was right. This *was* worse than being dumped. I had found a friend, but he lived in constant terror of being attacked by Tiger or Roy, and there was nothing I could do to help him.

CHAPTER 3

I watched until Tiger was completely out of view. Then I waited some more. I finally crawled closer to the fence. My back feet dragged along as I pulled with my front paws. I kept as low to the ground as I could.

"Why don't you run away?" I asked, pressing my nose against the fence.

"How am I going to get out? They keep the gate locked even when they're here. Roy or Zack checks the fence every day to make sure there are no new holes under the chain link." Spike's tongue rubbed at the wounds on his side. His ears drooped where Tiger had chewed at them.

"There has to be a way out. Have you looked

at the whole fence?" I jumped to my feet and started to walk along the pen.

"Don't be silly," Spike scoffed. "They check and guard it all the time. You don't want to run into Roy anywhere. If you really have to look for yourself, you'd better wait until he goes home. Tiger can't get through the fence to get you, but he will let Roy or Zack know that you are out there. They'll come after you for sure. You're a lot better off right where you are." Spike started licking his front legs.

"When do they leave? I'll start looking as soon as they are gone." I perked my ears.

"You'll have to wait until it's almost dark," he answered. "Roy brings Zack here in that old truck that's parked by the front gate. It makes so much noise that you can hear them when they leave. Just keep your ears perked. You can't miss it."

"I know there has to be some way out of this big cage." I looked one way, then the other. "Maybe you could sneak out under their feet when they leave."

"I don't think so. I tried that once. They tied me up for two days. Don't really want to do

23

that again. I'm pretty tired right now." Spike groaned as he curled to one side.

"Don't worry, Spike. We'll figure a way out of this. There has to be something we can do to get you to safety."

"You're a pretty positive kind of dog for one that was dumped just this week. Get real. I'm trapped in and you're trapped out—neither one of us is living the good life. You'd better just hit the road as soon as they are gone. Don't look back. If you're lucky, somebody may take you in. You're a good-looking dog, somebody may want you. Just don't let it be Roy." Spike scrunched into a ball.

It seemed like forever before I finally heard the roar of the truck's engine. Spike barely twitched his ears.

I scampered to my feet. I didn't want to alert Tiger. Roy was gone, and the big, nasty bully could bark his head off, but no one would hear him. Tiger couldn't get out of the pen to get me, but he *could* hurt my friend.

I hadn't moved very far when Tiger strolled around the corner. He stood over Spike and snarled, "Get up, you worthless mangy dog. It's worktime, not naptime."

"I'm up. I'm going." Spike cautiously pulled himself to his feet. His legs trembled as he watched the ridge on Tiger's back bristle.

"You'd better do a good job. If it wasn't for me, they would have run you off a long time ago. I have to do my work and yours. Now go on. And keep that big white dog from coming back." Tiger towered over the frightened pup as he snorted his commands. "I heard you talking to him. Roy will try to turn him into a watchdog, and then there sure won't be enough to eat. Get moving!"

"I'm going. I'm going. I'll get my job done." Spike eased away from Tiger slowly. Tiger's legs were stiff and straight. His shoulders firm and rigid.

I crouched lower. I wanted to disappear into the ground. Tiger stared as Spike moved out of sight. Finally he kicked the dirt with his hind legs, turned, and walked the opposite way.

When my muscles finally relaxed, I crept along the fence, following in the direction that Spike had gone. When I spotted him, he was sitting near a pile of wood, scratching.

"Yip, yip. Spike, over here. Come here," I yelped softly to him.

"Are you still here? I thought you would have been long gone by now. Didn't you see what Tiger did to me? You'd better get on your way."

"No, I'm not leaving you. You're my friend. We're going to get you out of here somehow. We just need a plan, and I think I've got one. Keep patrolling. The next time you come this way, stop and I'll let you know what it is." I scooted away from the fence.

"Are you sure? This seems pretty hopeless to me. After a while you get kind of used to it."

"No, really. We can do it," I assured him. "I'm going to get you out. Just give me a few minutes. I think you're too short to jump over the fence, but there has to be a way."

"You really think so? I've been wanting to get out of here for a long time, but it hasn't happened yet. Like I said, I tried to get through the gate once and ended up tied with a chain. That was awful. You'd better go on. Save yourself!" Spike stared at me.

"We can do it. I just need some time to think." I licked the whiskers on the right side of my mouth, then nibbled at my bottom lip. I just had to come up with a plan. . . .

"Okay. I'll make a patrol. Will you be here?" Dust flew in the twilight as Spike shook himself.

I nodded my head so hard that my ears flopped.

"I'll be here."

I touched the fence and waited for Spike to get close enough to lick him with my tongue.

"I believe you will come up with a plan. Make sure you don't let Tiger see you. I'll be in big trouble if he knows you're still here." Spike licked at the fence.

I stayed hidden until Tiger finally patrolled back around. As soon as he was gone, I leaped up and ran to the fence. My plan would work. Digging. I was an excellent digger. I had dug out of my yard before. I had dug up the flowers at my old house. The gophers were always asking me to dig for them. This would work.

* * *

By the time Spike came by, I had a pile of dirt next to the fence. I was making progress.

"Hey, Freddie, what are you doing? Are you crazy? Tiger will see that pile so quick." Mouth gaping wide, Spike stared at the brown mound.

"No, that's where the plan comes in. You have to do your part, though." I snorted, to blow some of the dust from my nose.

Spike's tail tucked. "I'm telling you, Tiger's going to see that."

"That's where you come in. When he gets here, you're going to go running to him. Get him to go with you to the other side of the junkyard."

"How?"

"I don't know. Tell him that you heard something, or that something ran by. That way he won't have time to check this place out. It'll work. It's a good plan. I'll dig this whole part. When I finish, I'll go to the far side of the junkyard and yip at him or something. Then you start working on your side. He'll be so busy barking at me that you can get out. It'll work!" I grinned at him and wagged my tail.

"Sounds like a super plan, Freddie. Just one little thing."

"Yeah, it's great, isn't it? We've got to get busy! Go on patrol some more," I encouraged.

"No, you don't get it. I don't know how to dig!" Spike's jowls drooped.

My mouth flew open, and I blinked about three times.

"Can't dig? You're a dog. All dogs can dig."

"Not me. I tried. It doesn't work."

"Anybody can dig. You just put your paws out and burrow into the ground. You can do it." I looked him in the eye.

"I *can't* dig." Spike's head sagged low to the ground.

"You can do it. Gophers can dig. Even stupid cats can dig. Just put your paw out, and things will happen naturally." I stuck out my paw and started digging.

Spike moved closer to the fence. His eyes pierced into the dusk.

"Come on, get busy. We don't have time to mess around." I looked up briefly to see what Spike was doing.

It seemed like forever, but he finally tapped at the ground with his paw.

"You've got to put some backbone into it. Shove down with your claws, then pull back like you're going to get a sticker out. The topsoil may be hard, but it gets easier as you get farther down." I kept digging, but I watched from the corner of my eye.

Spike patted at the ground until he finally got some dirt out with one claw.

"I've got it! Look. We *can* do it." Spike's hind legs jumped around like crazy.

"Well, not quite, but it's a good try. Look, Spike, go take Tiger over to the other side. As soon as you can get away from him, hurry back here. I'll keep working. I think you can get the hang of it, but we don't want to get caught." I sniffed at him.

I dug and dug. Maybe this would be harder than I thought. I'd have to dig all of my side, then scoop under the fence as much as I could. Spike needed a lot of encouragement with his digging.

The opening under the fence was almost wide enough when Spike trotted back to me.

"Tiger is howling at some coyotes right now. He fell for that pretty easily. The coyotes helped. They were already yapping at a train whistle." Spike dropped his nose closer to the hole.

More dirt flew between my hind legs. "Get busy, Spike. We only have a little time. The coyotes won't keep him busy forever."

Spike sniffed the spot that he had started. His front feet patted the ground again. Suddenly he began slapping the dirt around like mad. Clods and dust flew everywhere. When he realized that he *was* moving down into the earth, he went crazy.

"Slow down a little, Spike. You're going to wear yourself out. Tiger's got to think you've been patrolling. He can't get suspicious yet."

"Oh, yeah. Hey, this is pretty fun. Wonder why I hadn't thought of it sooner? I could have been out of here long ago." Spike shook the dirt from his back.

"I don't know. Probably nobody ever showed you before. I had lots of good digging teachers at home. I'm almost finished with my side. When you get back, I'll go keep Tiger busy. Right now you'd better go check on him again. We're too far along to get caught now." I kept digging.

When Spike returned, my opening was perfect. I had dug under the fence and taken out enough dirt, so all he had to do was break through the surface.

"Tiger is clear on the other side of the yard, chasing a rat in the woodpile," Spike announced. "That should keep him occupied for a while. I'm ready to dig. Are we almost done?"

"Check it out. I have most of the dirt pulled from below you. All you have to do is dig down and break through to the big opening I made. Get after it, Spike!" I stood back a little.

"Here I go!" Spike started clawing into the earth. The dirt flew and hit the ground with a loud *swoosh* after *swoosh*.

I trotted to the far side of the junkyard. Ears perked, I listened for the big dog as I sneaked toward his patrol area. I heard him talking to the rat.

"Come on out, little guy. I know you're in there. I won't hurt you. Come see Tiger." The mean dog licked his lips as he rustled through some trash. I dropped to my stomach and watched as he sniffed and snorted through the pile.

Certain he was still busy, I headed back to Spike.

I was almost to our big trench when I heard Tiger yelp. Running as fast as I could, I got back to Spike. He was almost out! I jumped into the ditch and started digging from my side. We only needed another inch or so.

My sharp ears could hear Tiger coming toward us. Panting and puffing, the beast was moving closer and closer.

"Dig, Spike!" I yelped at him.

"I'm digging. I'm digging!" Dirt flew everywhere as we both clawed frantically.

For an instant I stopped digging and peeked up. The huge, mean dog lumbered toward us. His teeth shined yellow in the moonlight. His powerful jaws opened. His tight eyes aimed right at Spike's rear end.

CHAPTER 4

"Aarraug! I'll get you, you nasty little dog!"
Tiger slobbered as he charged toward Spike's
rear end.

"Take a deep breath and dive!" I yapped at
Spike. "You can make it!"

Twisting and turning, the little dog squeezed
himself into the hole. The end of his tail
flashed through just as Tiger's strong jaws
snapped shut.

The big, vicious dog stuck his nose into the
hole. Dropping to his elbows, he snorted at the
loose dirt. Wide-eyed, panting, and shaking,
Spike raced to stand beside me.

"You made it!" I said, kissing him on the

cheek with my tongue. "We did it. You're safe."

Spike looked back. Tiger sniffed the dirt and frowned. With a wag of his tail, my new friend trotted back to the fence. Right in front of Tiger, he turned around and kicked some clods at him with his hind feet.

"I'll get you for this!" Tiger snarled, burrowing into the dirt with his nose.

"No, you won't. You can't ever get me now. You're stuck in there *forever*, and I am free, free, free." Spike turned to me and wagged his tail. "I'm ready, Freddie, let's move out!"

"You're not going to get away with this," Tiger barked. "Roy will get you. He may even send *me* after you." Tiger charged at the fence. Sharp yellow teeth bit and tore at the wire.

Spike stuck his nose in the air. "Nah. He doesn't need me when he has a fine watchdog like you. Look what a great job you did, letting me escape. Besides, now there will be more food for you."

Tiger threw himself against the fence. Teeth bared, his growl grew more ferocious and angry.

"Come on, Spike. We'd better move on." I nudged at the little dog.

"No, this is too much fun. Tiger has been mean to me ever since I got here. He deserves it." Spike's tail flipped back and forth.

I nudged at Spike's rear again. "You're free. Don't be mean. That's not what you're about. Let's go."

"Yeah, I guess you're right. We've got to move on down the road." Spike prissed as we walked away. Tiger stayed even with us, stalking us from the other side of the fence.

Suddenly Tiger spun and ran back to the hole that we had dug. He started clawing at the dirt.

"Come on, Spike. We've got to run."

We sprinted away from the fence and headed for the trees. We ran and ran until we found a small pond. It was muddy and yucky looking, but it was still cool. We lapped the water. Just as I leaned down for another drink, something hit my rear. The force sent me staggering. I had to leap to keep from landing smack on my nose. Paddling for all I was worth, I turned around and swam back for the bank.

"Figured you needed a little dip." Spike's tail wagged so hard I thought he was going to knock his hind legs out from under him.

"You pushed me."

"Right." He nodded. "Look out. Here I come."

Spike sprang right over me and landed with a big splash in the water. Snapping and chewing at the waves, he swam all around before he came back to the bank where I stood.

"Come on. Let's swim down to the far end before we get out," he suggested. "That way, if Tiger *is* following us, it'll be harder for him to pick up our scent."

We dog-paddled to the far end of the little pond, climbed out, shook, then trotted down a dirt road to our right.

"You think he's going to get out of there?" Spike asked.

"No. He's a lot bigger than you are, and you just barely made it. It would take him forever to get the hole wide and deep enough."

Both of us were sure that Tiger wasn't following. Still . . .

* * *

When we first met, Spike tried to act mean. But his eyes were soft and gentle, and even when he growled I could tell he was a nice dog at heart. Tiger . . . well, he was a different matter. He was mean. Not only was he mean, he *liked* being mean. When I thought of his big, sharp, yellow teeth, and his narrow eyes, and the way his lips curled at the sides when he tore into Spike . . . well, my feet just kind of went faster.

"If he does get out, he may take off for freedom," Spike said, more to himself than to me.

"When was the last time he was out of the yard?" I asked.

"I don't *ever* remember him being out. Once you get in that place, you just don't leave."

I don't know how far or how long we traveled, when Spike stopped.

"Hey, what are those lights?" he asked, pointing his nose toward two bright spots.

"Must be a car. Get over to the side. Looks like it's really moving."

"You think it's Roy and Zack?" Spike pressed against me.

"No, but we'd better get over. That guy is

moving fast." I nudged Spike toward the side of the road.

Dirt and rocks showered us as the car zoomed past and down the road. Taillights glowed red as we watched the back of the car disappear into the dark.

"Let's get off this road," I suggested. "I need a nap. Let's head for that thicket." I looked both ways before we stepped across the road. "We'll slip through those trees. If we find a pond or a creek, we can cut through it. That way our scent will change if anybody does come looking for us."

"I'm with you, pal. We need to watch out in here, though. Sometimes the sound of coyote howls that we hear at night comes from this direction. I don't want to meet any of those guys. I've been talking trash to them for a long time. They may recognize my sound and turn us into mush." Spike moved closer to me as we entered the trees.

We had only gone a little ways when he stopped again. "This is far enough." He dropped his nose closer to the ground and sniffed. "Smells safe. Let's sleep here." Spike walked around in circles, patting the grass down for a bed. Suddenly he stopped. His ears perked straight up and he leaned to one side. "Look, Freddie. Isn't that water over there?"

The tall trees in the forest blocked most of the moonlight. I squinted, trying to see what he was talking about. In the distance there was an open spot with no trees or brush. Moonlight glistened and sparkled off something.

"Yeah, I think I see it." We walked toward it with our ears perked, listening for sounds of other animals that might be close by.

Sure enough, it was a pond. It was long and wide. Moonlight danced and shimmered across the surface. We lapped the cold water for a moment, then leaped in.

"This is great!" Spike bit at the smooth water. Ripples turned into waves as the little dog got more excited. He shook his head back and forth. Sprays of white sloshed into the night air.

"Spike, stop. Listen." Ears perked, I tried to recognize a new sound that moved toward us. I just couldn't quite make out what it was.

"Honk, honk, honk!"

We both paddled for the edge of the pond. Once the soft mud was under my feet, I turned to keep an eye on the water as I backed up and eased closer to the bank. "Spike, listen. There is something in here with us!"

"Yip! Yowie!" Spike yelped as he splashed out of the water and bounded high up onto the bank.

"Honk! Honk! Get away from our pond!"

Wings spread, three huge birds suddenly rose up from the water and loomed over me.

"Chill!" Spike barked from the safety of the bank. "What was all that about? Why did you nip me on the tail? We weren't doing anything."

One of the birds swam closer to me. The other two headed for Spike. I backed up a bit more.

"You're in *our* pond. Get out! Get away from our babies," the big bird hissed. "We have families to protect. Go on!"

I was surprised how quiet and fast the birds swam up on us. It was even more of a shock to see how fast they moved once they were out of the water. The two splashed and sloshed onto the bank after Spike. He yipped again when one nipped his tail with her beak. A long neck stretched out toward me. I spun and took off. The beak kept snapping right at my tail when I sprang from the water and raced to join my friend, high up on the bank.

"What were those things?" Spike panted.

"Geese." I glanced behind us to make sure they weren't still following. Two of the shapes glided across the water, back to where they had been. "My boy and I used to see them when we went for walks in the park. He would give them pieces of bread, and they would follow us all over. When he finished feeding them, they would chase us. They can peck pretty hard. We need to move on even though I don't think they will come after us. They have babies to protect."

The thought of my boy and the fun we used to have made the sadness tug at my heart. Suddenly the goose who had chased me from the pond spread his wings and charged. The sadness was forgotten. I spun and took off with Spike right behind me.

"I was just starting to have fun in there." Spike shook his wet fur.

"Me, too."

My ears perked as we trotted through the tall trees and away from the lake. As we neared a field at the far edge of the forest, I heard a new sound.

"What is that?" Spike asked, tilting his head to one side.

"Cows."

"Cows?"

"Yeah. They are these big animals that eat grass."

"Are they dangerous?"

"No," I answered with a shrug of my ears. "They just stand around and eat and swish flies with their tails. They're big. I guess they could be dangerous if they stepped on you. If we're quiet, maybe we can slip through without bothering them."

We tucked our tails and quietly eased our way out into the opening. The big creatures stood very still, some with their heads up, some with their heads down. They must have been asleep on their feet. We crept along silently. Spike stayed right in my footsteps. At least I thought he did.

By the time I realized he wasn't following me, it was too late.

"Hey, look, Freddie," Spike's bark knifed through the night. "This guy is just about the same size as us. Isn't he cute?"

My eyes flashed wide. "Spike!" I gasped. "Get away from him, now!"

"Moooooo." The sound that came from the little animal was more like a cry than a bellow. It was all it took.

"Mooo rooow!" Suddenly a big cow stood, glaring down at Spike. "Get away from my baby."

Then, before I knew what was happening, there was more mooing and bellowing than I had ever heard in my life. The very ground seemed to shake beneath my feet as the whole herd rushed toward us.

In the blink of an eye we were surrounded. The enormous animals towered above us. Their soft brown eyes were so tight and filled with anger that they seemed to glow red in the moonlight.

We were in big trouble!

CHAPTER 5

Spike and I backed up until our rear ends bumped together. Then we backed up even farther, until we were practically sitting on each other's rumps. All around us cows snorted and bellowed. Pitching their big heads toward the sky, they kept stepping closer and closer. With each step, we pressed harder against each other, until we were almost a ball.

"Hey, Spike, we've got to get out of here," I whispered, shoving him toward the trees. Spike didn't move.

"Sounds great, but how? That one has really sharp things on his head. Looks like the poky sticks they used on me at the junkyard."

I took a deep breath. "Get ready. When I say go, stay low and head for the trees. These guys are big, but they aren't as fast as we are. Just keep running."

"I don't know. They're everywhere!" Spike shivered and pressed even harder against my bottom.

"Just take off, and don't look back. Ready? GO!" I barked.

Spike leaped forward so quick, and I was leaning against him so hard . . . well, I almost fell over backward. I managed to catch myself and spin around to follow as he raced into the circle of cows. I was hot on his heels. I stayed so close that his tail kept flopping me in the nose as we ran.

Dodging and darting, we wove between twenty cow legs. An enormous hoof flashed at the corner of my eye. I ducked and leaned to the left. Just in time! The hard hoof was so close it brushed my whiskers but didn't hit my head.

A huge head ducked at me. I heard the sharp point slice through the air. The horns just missed my back. Slobbers from the mouth landed against my side. The snorting and mooing was so loud, it was like a wall of noise. How we managed to escape and make it to the brush . . . I still don't know.

We ran and ran and ran until we could hardly breathe.

"We can stop now, Spike," I wheezed.

"Nah, let's keep going," he panted. "I don't want to see those guys again. They may get us if we slow down."

"We can go a little farther." I had to pause and suck in another breath. "But they should be settling down for the night. We need to get some rest, too."

We ran a while longer, then slowed to a trot. Finally we walked. We were well clear of the cow pasture when we finally found a safe place to sleep.

The rest of the night was uneventful. When we awoke the next morning, we found about five different trails that branched out from near the spot where we rested. We sniffed at each of them. Some were well traveled, some not. I didn't want to cross paths with anyone unexpectedly, so we trotted down the path that had the least traffic.

"What's for breakfast, Freddie?" Spike asked after a while.

"I haven't seen a thing. No garbage dump or trash can. No place where people throw things away. We may have to chow down on grasshoppers."

"Yummy, my favorite!" Spike's nose curled to a disgusted sneer. "I'm thinking I should have stayed at the junkyard. This isn't working out very well."

He stopped to scratch at one of his fleas. I turned back and stood beside him.

"I thought we'd see a house by now, too. I just can't believe we haven't—"

A sudden noise made me stop right in the middle of what I was saying. My ears stood straight up. Spike's did, too.

"Do you hear that?"

"It's another dog, isn't it?"

"I think so." I nodded. "And if it's a dog, there has to be food for him to eat."

"Let's go find out," Spike said with a wag of his tail.

"We'd better be careful. He may be like Tiger or worse," I cautioned.

"Thanks for reminding me about Tiger." Spike's head drooped and his tail stopped wagging.

The barking sound led us to a little hill. We flattened ourselves on the ground and crawled on our bellies to peek over the top. Below us, in a little valley, we saw a house with a short wooden fence around it. The dog was barking at something in a tree.

"He looks pretty big to me, Freddie. Not as big as you, but he looks old, and mean, and cranky, and . . . and . . ."

The barking stopped and the dog ran to the fence and looked our way.

"Grrrr ooow! Stay away from here." He snarled as he bounced against the fence.

"This isn't the right place for us, Spike. We'd better move on." I slowly backed away from my perch on the hill.

The next house looked friendly, until a thin man came running out of it, yelling at the top of his voice.

"Get out of here, you mongrels!"

Spike and I tucked our tails, but we didn't run away.

"I mean it! Go on, get!" He waved his arms in the air.

"Let's go a little closer, it may be okay." I dropped and wagged my tail. "Maybe if I look sweet and friendly . . ."

"Oh, I see how it is." The man turned and marched back into the house.

"Maybe he's going for some food." Spike's tail wagged.

We sat still for just a few seconds. All at once my eyes flashed wide when I saw the shiny metal stick in his hands.

"No, I don't think so," I yelped. "Run, Spike! Run for your life!"

Kaaa-blam!!!

Tiny lead pellets peppered the grass and weeds, just inches behind our rumps.

"I guess he means business," Spike said when we finally stopped running and cowered near some bushes.

"Yeah, he's serious, but he shot behind where we were. I don't think he really wanted to hurt us."

"Yeah, right." Spike huffed. "Just his way of telling us to go away."

"Right." I shrugged my ears.

Spike licked his front paw. "We have to find something. Maybe a road with more cars? People throw food out all the time. Meat, bread, other stuff."

"Yum, that sounds almost as good as grasshoppers." Just the thought made my tongue rub against the roof of my mouth, like I was trying to get rid of some nasty taste or something.

Spike nudged at my head. "Come on. Let's give it a try."

The road wasn't any good, either. Every piece of paper was just a smell. No bites of food, not even a crumb. So—it was back to the field and—grasshoppers. They were crunchy and full of protein. But the taste wasn't exactly what I'd call yummy.

Exhausted and still hungry, we found some dried grass near a plum patch. We walked around in circles, patting it down to make our bed.

"I'll keep first watch." I arched my neck to check the area.

"Okay. I'm pretty tired." Spike rolled himself into a ball, but managed to still touch me at the same time. His eyes closed and he was sound asleep. I listened to the noises around me. I don't know what happened, but I must have dozed off, too.

"*Woof, woof, grrr, woof, woof.*" Soft barking sounds woke me up.

My eyes popped open and I looked around. Spike was on his back, his feet in the air. He was as relaxed as could be. He was still asleep, but he was barking and growling at something.

"*Woof, woof, grrr, woof, woof,*" he yipped again.

I jumped up and looked down at him. "Wake up, Spike, you're dreaming."

"Huh? What?" The little dog flipped over and struggled to his feet. "What?"

"You're dreaming, dog. Barking and growling at something. It must have been pretty scary." I nuzzled him.

"Can't remember anything." Spike yawned. He blinked a couple of times and shook his head. "It couldn't have been too bad."

"Lie back down. Try to get some sleep," I said.

"That's easy for you to say. I *was* asleep and you woke me up to tell me I was sleeping. That doesn't make any sense. Now you tell me to get some sleep. Besides that, I'm hungry." Spike scratched his head with his front paw.

"Yeah." I sighed. "Me, too. We should be able to find something tomorrow." I snuggled up against Spike.

My ears suddenly stood up on end. "Do you hear that?"

Spike twisted his head, listening to the scratching sounds in the grass. We both stared into the dark. The sound came closer.

"What is it?" Spike whispered. "I can't see anything."

"I don't know, but I think it's coming this way."

As we peered into the night, two creatures rustled out from some tall grass and into a little clearing. Long snouts scraped the ground in front of them.

"I can't see anything." Spike sat up on his haunches and stared at the brush. "What is it?"

My eyes flashed wide.

"What is it?" he repeated.

My eyes just got bigger and bigger, but I couldn't answer.

"Freddie," Spike snapped. "What is it?"

"Don't know. They're not bobcats or coyotes. The things are really weird. They have a long pointy nose on one end, little pig ears, and a hard covering—kind of like . . . like . . . well, I don't know what it's like. It's all over their bodies. Then there's this long pointy tail and . . . I've never see anything like it."

"Scoot over, let me see." Spike shoved me aside with his shoulder.

"Maybe we'd better just get out of here." I scooted farther in the other direction.

Spike's tail started to wag. "No, it's okay. These guys are funny. Just watch. They get scared really easy." Slow and quiet, he moved toward them.

The big animals dug and burrowed into the soft earth, never looking up. I was careful to keep Spike between me and the weird creatures.

Spike crept out of the bushes and crouched down in the path of the animals. The two big things moved slowly toward him. Snouts down along the ground, they sniffed and rooted in the leaves. Spike was perfectly still as they moved nearer. Well, almost. His tail flipped just a bit, and his whole rear end wiggled back and forth. Ears perked, he almost seemed to tremble with excitement. The two animals were so busy concentrating on sniffing the leaves and dirt that they didn't even see him. Their noses almost touched when Spike suddenly jumped up on all fours.

"Grrrrrr. Get! Get out of here!" Spike barked furiously.

Eyes and mouths as wide as could be, the two big creatures stared blankly at Spike. Then—before I could even blink—they jumped straight up, spun around in midair, and bounded back into the brush. I blinked a couple of times. It was hard to believe something that clunky looking—heavy and all covered with a hard shell—could move that fast. Long tails dragged behind their hard backs as they scooted out of sight.

Spike and I laughed as the two animals disappeared.

"What were those things? How did you know they would run away?" I stared into the dark brush.

"Those are armadillos. They're pretty harmless to us. They used to come around the junkyard at night. They dig in the dirt for insects to eat. The best part is that they scare so easily. Did you ever see anything as funny as those guys? I'll bet they are still scooting through the field." Spike was laughing so hard he had trouble standing on all four legs.

"*Grrrrrowl!*"

The sound came from behind us. The hair on the back of my neck stood straight up.

"What are you two bag of bones doing in *our* forest?" Deep voices came from the trees.

Not blinking. Not even breathing. Spike and I spun around and stood plastered together as the voices came closer.

CHAPTER 6

"Let's get 'em, boys!" Sharp white teeth shone in the moonlight as the creatures moved closer.

"We're not doing anything, leave us alone," I pleaded.

"*You* don't have to do anything, we'll do it all." The mangy-looking coyote licked his lips and leered at us.

"Yeah, relax. We know what we're doing." Another one of the beasts ambled closer.

I shook so hard, I thought my tail was going to fall off—then my paws and then my legs. Spike just stood beside me. His tail wagged, slow and easy, like he didn't have a care in the world. I took a deep breath and tried to act brave.

"Listen, guys, we're just passing through. We aren't here to cause you any trouble. We're leaving, okay?" Fluffing up my fur, I tried to look as big as I could.

"We know what you are doing. We've been watching you." The biggest coyote stepped to his right, closer to me.

I stood my ground but I could hear my stomach grumbling. "Then you know that we're not here to cause you any trouble."

"Trouble. You dogs are always trouble. Right now you're trying to get our food." The coyote flipped one ear. His fur was drab and dirty.

Two more coyotes moved in from the trees. None of them looked any better than the first two. Hunger still gnawed at my insides. I felt weak and tired and scared, as I tried to pretend to be strong and brave. There were four of them, small but wily, and they knew their way around the country. There were only two of us, one big, one little. I had been in some dog scuffles in town. Usually, I could talk my way out of them. For some reason, these guys looked and acted a lot different from town dogs.

"Come on, gang, let's get them." They circled closer.

Spike just smiled at them.

I heard a gulping sound when I swallowed. "Hey, guys, let's talk this over. I'm bigger than three of you put together. My pal here—he's a junkyard dog. The toughest kind of dog in the world. You know that. Junkyard dogs are mean and vicious. They just don't get any worse." I looked at Spike. "Look mean," I whispered.

Spike just wagged his tail.

Suddenly the coyotes stopped.

"Junkyard dog?"

I nodded my head so fast and hard that my ears flopped. "Yeah. Junkyard dog."

The big coyote puffed out his chest. "I don't believe it. He doesn't look tough enough to be a junkyard dog. What's your name?"

"Look mean," I urged my friend again.

Spike ignored me. He strolled toward the coyotes, as if they were nothing more than harmless puppies. The four animals sneered at him. Almost to where they stood, Spike sat on his rump and scratched at a flea.

"I don't like to be called 'The Junkyard Dog.'" He gnawed at the flea with his teeth. "It's not a very pretty name. I like my real name better."

The smallest of the four coyotes took a step back.

"What is your name?"

Spike yawned and stretched. I felt my eyes flash wide when he lay down, right in front of them. They could pounce on him. They could be all over him faster than a hummingbird's wings could flap. There was no way I could fight them by myself. What in the world . . .

"You don't happen to know a coyote by the name of Lop, do you?" Spike rubbed his cheek against the ground. "I met him one time. Always wondered what happened to old Lop."

All four of the coyotes took steps backward.

"What's your name?" the big one asked in a muffled growl.

Suddenly Spike was on his feet. He puffed himself up and wagged his tail. He was twice as big as usual.

"You know me already, don't you, fellows."

Spike looked amazing. His eyes narrowed to tiny black dots, and his fur stood up in a ragged ridge down his back.

"You're not . . . not . . . you're not *Tiger*, are you?"

Spike's tail fanned the breeze. "I always wanted to meet up with old Lop again," he said. "I didn't really mean to get his ear." Spike smiled so big his teeth glistened. "I was trying to get his whole head in my mouth. You don't know where I could find him, do you? Are you guys related to him by any chance?"

The coyotes spun around and took off. Only problem, they had eased closer and closer together as they watched Spike. When they tried to run, all they could do was bump into one another. They crashed and thumped and bumped, managing to end up in a tangled pile of paws and tails. Snouts snapping, frightened voices yapping, they rolled and tumbled on the ground.

Then . . . they were gone. The only thing left was a cloud of dust that swirled around us, then drifted off into the night.

Mouth wide, I looked at Spike again. His fur

was down and his eyes were soft again.

"What in the world? How did you do that?" I asked.

"Don't know. I really don't know. Coyotes come around the junkyard all the time. They come to the fence and try to get our food. They can't get in, so Tiger always talks real ugly to them. He got that one called Lop, by the ear, one time. I think that's why they named him Lop—because he only has one ear and he looks kind of lopsided. Anyway, after that they never got near the fence again. Coyotes do a lot of howling. Guess word got around, real quick, about Tiger."

"How did you manage to act so cool and calm? Weren't you scared?"

"Sure I was scared," Spike admitted. "But I couldn't let *them* know that. I had to make them believe I was Tiger and ready to eat them up."

Just watching him and thinking how fast the cowardly coyotes took off, I felt brave as could be. "Hey, I think we could have taken them. You're pretty big and strong and—"

"Forget it!" Spike interrupted, shivering. "We have to get out of here. They might come back." We took off in the opposite direction from the coyotes.

We kept our pace for a mile or so before we stopped for a quick dog nap. It was getting light when we woke up. With both of our tummies growling, we headed back toward the road.

We hadn't been walking very long when we had to make another decision. Our road turned into gravel and dust. We either had to head back toward the town or keep looking in the country.

"There's more people in town, so that means more food. Houses aren't very close around here." I sat and stared at Spike.

"That's all true, but more people might recognize me. Then they'd send for Roy and Zack if we go back toward town. Let's take our chances in the country. I really don't want to go back to the junkyard." Spike jumped up. "Ready, Freddie?"

We were dog trotting when we sighted another farmhouse. We crouched down and watched for a long time. We could see a big fence surrounding the yard behind the house.

Another fence divided that, making a smaller pen. There were two wooden doghouses there, and instead of green grass, the area was mostly dirt.

"Yip, yip!" Friendly sounds came from the smaller pen.

"Look, Freddie. There's a couple of dogs. They look big, but they sound rather nice. Don't you think so?" Spike started to get up.

"Keep your seat, Spike Dog, let's watch a little longer." I didn't want to take any more chances. We needed to save all of our strength just in case we had to walk some more.

Wagging their tails, the dogs watched us. After yipping an invitation to us, they would walk around their pen and sit down. Stomachs growling, we finally decided to check the place out.

As we got closer the two dogs stood up to get a better look at us. Their tails whipped back and forth so fast, they almost knocked each other down.

"Hey, come closer. We can't get out, but we want to meet you." The two dogs sniffed at us through the fence.

They were about the same size. One was a pointer bird dog, the other one . . . I wasn't sure. She was black, but she was getting gray around the face. Her hair was pretty short and her long tail was just a little furry.

"Hey, what took you two so long? We've been waiting for you." The black dog stuck the tip of her nose through one of the chain-link squares.

"Waiting for us? What for?" Puzzled, I stepped even closer to the fence.

"We haven't had a . . ."

Before she could finish, a man strolled around the side of the barn. The instant he saw us, he bent over and picked up a big stick from the ground. Shaking the thing at us, he yelled at the top of his voice:

"Get out of here! Go on. You two have to go. Scat! You can't stay here."

Spike was in front of me as we charged for some nearby trees. Behind us, we heard the girl dog barking.

"Wait. Don't leave," she yapped. "He doesn't really mean it."

"That was close." Spike panted. "That man

didn't look very friendly, but the dog said they were waiting for us. What do you think she meant?"

"I don't know. Just keep going. We can rest behind those rocks." I nudged Spike.

After we caught our breath and settled down for a few minutes, I jumped up and started sniffing. Rocks were piled up on mounds of dirt. It seemed strange to me, and I didn't recognize the smells that came to my nose.

"Get over here, Freddie! There's somebody coming. It doesn't look like the crazy guy with the stick, but we'd better hide anyway." Spike huddled behind a stack of rocks. I snuggled down next to him to watch.

"Pup. Here, pup. Come on, I know you're here somewhere," a soft voice called out.

"Bethany, come back here! They're gone now. We don't *need* another dog! Besides that there were two of them." A deep voice called after her. "I'll have to get a second job just to buy the dog food we'll need. Come back . . . please."

"Oh, Andy, how much could two little dogs eat?"

"Plenty. That one dog is huge. I'll bet he can eat a bag a week. Please come back," the man begged.

The woman just giggled at him.

"He's got to be starving then. Big dog, little dog, hungry dogs. We've got to feed them." She moved closer to our hiding place.

"We already have four dogs." The man sighed. "We're not a dog shelter. They probably have ticks and fleas. Let them go."

The woman's soft hazel eyes seemed to light up when she spotted us. "I can see them. Come here, Andy. Look how cute they are."

"Jake and Ding were cute when you let them stay," the man grumped. He reached out for the woman's arm.

"Jake and Ding are still cute," she snapped, pulling her arm away. "I love them. You know they are wonderful dogs. They make me laugh every day." With a smile, she turned, grabbed the man, and gave him a big hug.

"What about Biff and Barkie? They are *not* cute." The man tried to look angry and disgusted, but all he could do was smile.

"I know they're not the prettiest dogs in the

world. But they are old and I love them, too. Pugs can't help it. Besides, Biff was your mother's favorite." She kissed him on the cheek.

"Oh, my gosh. I'm running a dog circus here, right?" The man patted her on the head.

"I guess. Come on and help me get these pups fed. After they eat, perhaps they'll leave. They may just be hungry." The woman hugged him again.

"I'm pretty sure you said that with Jake and Ding! As a matter of fact, I'm positive. Oh, well . . . I might as well get this over with. I'll get the pans. See if you can get them over here." The man kissed her on the head and shuffled back toward the house.

"Here, puppies. Come on, we'll get some food and water for you. Come on." The woman crouched down, reached out her arms, and wiggled her fingers at us.

I perked both ears.

"What are you thinking, dog?" Spike growled soft in his throat. "You don't know her, or him. How can you trust them?" The fur ruffled on his back.

I felt my tail wag as I watched the woman and her gentle smile. "Sometimes, you just have to take a chance." I sighed. "She looks really nice. He can't be too bad. And besides, what about Jake and Ding over there? They said they were waiting for us." I looked at the two dogs standing by their fence. Their tails wagged and wagged.

"Come on, you two. Let's get some food." The woman moved closer and touched the top of my head. Spike stood tall and let out a timid growl.

"Relax, Spike. I'm starving. She's going to feed us. If we don't want to stay, we'll leave. We're hungry and she's offering food. Think about it." I shoved my nose under her hand.

"Good dog. What a sweetie." She rubbed my ears and face.

"How can you trust *people*? You loved your boy and you got dumped. Now you're going to trust these humans? You don't even know them. I think we'd better go." Spike's fur was still in a ridge across his back.

"Listen, Spike Dog. You know a lot of things, but I am hungry. Get it? Free food. No grasshoppers. No garbage." I woofed at Spike. Wagging my tail, I looked up at the lady. She scratched my ears and stood up.

"Come on, pups. Let's find Andy and get some dog food. It's okay. You're safe here."

The bird dog and the one named Ding put their paws on the fence and wagged their tails as we came closer.

"Welcome," the old black dog greeted. "We're glad you're here. What took you so long?"

"How did you know we were coming?" I asked the yapping dogs.

"We knew you were in the neighborhood." The bird dog barked at us. "Most strays who come around this area usually end up here."

"How did you know we were around?" Spike lifted his ears and tilted his head to one side.

"We heard the coyotes talking about you," the bird dog answered with a wag of his tail. "You must have crossed their path last night and—"

"But why did you think we'd come here?" The ridge on Spike's back smoothed down a bit.

"It just happens. Ding ended up here. I ended

up here. Just something about the place and the people . . . I guess. I'm not sure. Something draws dumped dogs."

Tail drooped and still cautious, Spike trotted slowly behind the woman and me.

"I'm still not sure about this," he complained.

"Here it is, Bethany." The man handed two bowls to the woman. "Your collection of dogs is getting out of hand. But here's food for these two barkers."

"Thank you, dear. Look at them. They are starving. I'll let them eat. If they need to go on their way, they can. If not, we'll try to find a good home for them." Bethany set one bowl down in front of me.

"I'm *so* sure they are going to run off as soon as they eat," the man teased. "Life around here is just too easy. That's why they leave—right? Of all the dogs that we've ever had, you've only found new homes for two. Your mother took one and Mr. McDonald took the other. I know what's going to happen. But I love you anyway." He set the other bowl down near Spike. When he reached to pat him on the head, Spike shied away.

Standing up, the man and woman backed toward the house.

I didn't wait. My stomach growled with anticipation as I slurped and gobbled the delicious food.

CHAPTER 7

"I guess I *was* pretty hungry," Spike mumbled, his mouth full of food.

"I think you got that right. It seems like a long time ago that my boy fed me. This is just as good. No, this is better." I woofed down the last few bites.

Bethany and Andy sat on the porch and watched us as we finished our yummy meal. They didn't say anything when we sprawled out under a big tree for a nap. They just got up quietly and went inside the house.

"What do you think, Freddie? Are we safe here?" Spike stretched his front legs out as far as he could. His rump wiggled back and forth as he flipped his tail.

"The food is excellent," I said, licking my front paws. "The people are nice. The other dogs seem happy and they like it here. We're far enough away from the junkyard that I don't think anyone is going to come looking for you."

"It's almost too perfect. Great food. Friendly people. Pleasant dogs. Too perfect." Spike closed his eyes and drifted off to sleep.

I watched for a while, but my eyelids felt heavy. I needed a little rest. Spike and I had walked a long way. For the first time in three days, our tummies were full. A short nap would be perfect.

"Hey, Pupper."

The voice startled me from my nap. My legs tensed, but before I could jump up and run, the woman's soft face smiled down at me.

"We're going for a walk. I don't suppose you two want to go."

My eyes blinked a couple of times and my tail flipped, just a bit, at the warmth of her voice. She held a very small dog in one arm. The man held another one. Both dogs' tongues hung out. I guess that was because their faces were smushed and flat. There probably wasn't enough room in their mouths to keep their tongues inside. Spike woke up with a growl.

"We're taking a walk. You two can stay here or go with us. Your choice." Bethany reached over to touch Spike.

He jumped to his feet and hopped out of reach.

Bethany shrugged. "We're not going far, but we're letting Jake and Ding out. They'll probably want to check you over. Just wanted to let you know."

Andy turned and walked toward the old black dog and the pointer. "I'll get them." Opening the gate, he headed for the pen where the two dogs were. The bird dog jumped straight up in the air as Andy came closer.

My mouth flopped wide and I blinked. The bird dog jumped again. He didn't even run or so much as bend his legs. He just jumped. All fours left the ground at the same time and he went straight up. The big thing hopped so high, he was almost even with the top of the fence. Again and again and again, he bounded into the air. I felt my eyes roll inside my head. It was weird. How could he do that? No matter how closely I watched, his legs barely bent as he popped up into the air. His big floppy ears floated out like the wings of a bird as he came down, only to hop again.

"Woo woo woof!" The black dog bounced toward the gate. She didn't jump like the bird dog. Her hind legs were stiff and could only move with short, tiny steps.

Andy opened the gate and scooted aside.

"Watch it! Here they come."

The two big dogs ran toward us. The white dog started sniffing at me. His nose whiffed so hard it almost sucked in some of my fur. The old black dog finally hobbled her way up to Spike. He bristled, then relaxed when he knew she was friendly.

"Jake! Ding!" Andy shouted. "Come on, let's go. You know the routine." He set the little dog in his arms onto the ground.

The old black dog turned and headed away from us, trotting at low speed.

"Woof! Be back!" The bird dog raced away so fast he left tiny clouds of dust floating in the air.

Even though he wasn't mad or scared, Spike's fur still stood on a ridge down his back. "What was that about?" he asked, crossing his eyes and shaking his head. "And where are they going?"

"I don't know. Want to go with them and find out?" I stood up and checked the food bowl again.

"Let's just hang out here and see what happens. I'm still pretty tired, aren't you?" Spike asked, finally relaxing the ridge of hair down his back.

Although Bethany and Andy carried them home, the two little dogs looked exhausted. Their legs dangled down and their tongues hung out, even farther than before.

"I'll put Biff and Barkie inside," Andy said, taking the two little dogs into the house.

"Come on Jake, Ding. Time to eat," Bethany called, opening their gate.

The bird dog ran to the water bowl. He put

his front paws in the big black bowl and started digging. It was like he was unearthing a bone or something, but he was jabbing at the water instead of the dirt. He dug so hard and fast, it took only seconds for his chest and belly to get totally soaked with the droplets and spray. I guess Bethany and Ding knew his routine. They both waited outside the gate until he shook and threw water all over the pen and the side of the doghouse. When he was finished, Bethany knelt down beside the black dog and rubbed Ding's ears and face. Then she stroked her back and legs. Ding leaned against the woman as she massaged her old shoulders and neck. After a few minutes she fluffed the dog's head one last time.

"Okay. It's time to eat."

Ding gave a shake and lumbered into the pen. She got a big drink before going to her food bowl.

Spike and I stood outside the backyard, watching. Bethany latched the smaller pen where Ding and Jake lived. Then she strolled to the gate where we stood. "Now, what about you two? Are you ready to join us in the backyard or are you still happy out here?" she asked, rubbing each one of my ears, then fluffing the hair on my back. She reached for Spike, but he backed away from her. Bethany stood up. "Not ready yet? It's okay, take your time."

"Don't you want to go in the yard?" I looked at Spike. The hair was up on his back again.

"How can you trust her?" Spike kicked at the dirt. "You don't know anything about these people. You were dumped not very long ago, and here you are, ready to jump into these people's arms. I don't get it."

"I can't sit around and hide. Bethany seems kind and I like her. I just have to see what happens. Besides, I don't like sleeping out in the wild. We were lucky bluffing the coyotes. They may not bluff the next time. You—Spike Dog—need to relax. This could be the best thing that ever happened to you. If you keep acting mean, you might miss it."

I plopped on the ground. Spike's lip curled and his whiskers raised up on one side of his mouth.

"You're cute and fluffy. Big—but cute. I'm just a junkyard dog. They will keep you and send me on my way. What will I do then?" Spike lay down and dropped his head to rest on his outstretched paws.

"You've had some hard times, Spike. Remember what your life was like before you went to the junkyard. That wasn't so bad, was it?"

"No, it was a very good time."

"Then don't worry," I said, thumping my tail against the ground. "We'll just see what happens. If things don't turn out well, we'll just travel some more. Is that okay with you?"

"I guess." With his chin resting on his paws, Spike's nose was so close to the ground that a puff of grass and dust spun up when he sighed. "Let's catch a nap. We'll wait and see. I guess we *are* due for something good, right, Freddie?"

"Right, Spike."

We spent the rest of the day under the trees in the front yard. That night we could hear coyotes howling in the valley. We slept, curled together in a pile, close to the porch.

The sky was just beginning to brighten when

85

Bethany let Biff and Barkie out the front door. Spike jumped up and ruffed his back. I stood up to greet them. They were running as fast as their little legs would carry them.

"Grrrrr. Get back. Give us some space," Spike rumbled the warning, deep in his throat.

"Space? *You're* in *our* space." Biff sniffed at my legs. Then he walked right under me. I nudged him with my nose, then I stretched out on the ground.

"Yeah. This is our home. We were here first. We can sniff all we want." Barkie stared straight into my eyes.

"Hey! Leave them alone." Bethany scolded as she trotted into the yard. "They aren't ready for you two, so early in the morning." She gently shoved Biff back with her foot as she lifted Barkie up into her arms.

She carried the chubby little dog to another part of the yard. The instant his feet touched the ground, Barkie began to sniff the grass. Biff ran to him, trying to sniff and find out if he had discovered some new smells on the ground. The little dogs took turns trailing each other.

Bethany knelt down between Spike and me.

"What are you two sweeties doing?"

Spike eased away as Bethany reached to rub his ears.

I liked being rubbed. If Spike didn't, that was his problem. I jumped up and leaned against Bethany. With a little giggle, she started stroking my head. She massaged my neck, then my shoulders. After that she scratched my back and sides.

"Hey, you two!" Suddenly she jumped up and ran to the fence where the little dogs were digging. "Let's go in. I don't have time to fill up holes."

I watched as she carried one of the little dogs and scooted the other one with her foot. The door shut behind them.

"Those little dogs look funny and they act so mean for little squirts." Spike moved closer again.

"Ah, they're okay. They're pretty curious, and I don't think they really want to harm anybody. They have to act tough. They were here first and they *are* inside dogs. Those two don't know anything about what it's like to be out in the real world." I stretched out in the sun.

* * *

The sunlight was warm on my fur. I don't know how long I slept. The sound of Jake's barking woke me up. Spike hopped to his feet and started looking all around.

"It's the bird dog. Something must be bothering him. Let's go see." I shook my woolly coat as I stood up.

The pen that held Jake and Ding was on the back edge of Bethany and Andy's yard. Skirting the outside of the fence, we walked closer. The dog was barking at something in the tree. He wouldn't stop. Ding couldn't care less. She was stretched out in the dirt near a doghouse.

"Hey, what are you barking at?" I asked the big dog.

"Uh? What?" Jake turned to look at us.

"What are you barking at? I don't see anything in that tree." I stared up at the branches.

"Oh, it's just that obnoxious squirrel. He comes in here about twice a day. I would appreciate it if he would get his own tree. As a matter of fact, he has a whole grove over there. Acorns, pecans—any kind of tree he could possibly want. This old tree barely has leaves.

Why he wants to come in here and stare down at us, I'll never know. Besides that, I just need to bark sometimes. He rattles those leaves and I just can't help it." Jake slurped from his water bowl.

"Why don't you get to run in the big backyard?" Spike's nose touched the fence.

"I don't really know." Jake shook his head. His ears flopped.

"You *do* know, Jake." Ding stood up and stretched out her front legs.

"What? Oh, yeah. I guess I do." Jake pushed his nose through the wire, in the chain-link fence, to give us a sniff.

"Okay. I'll ask again," Spike said with a jerk of his tail. "Why don't you get to run around in the whole backyard? It looks really nice on the other side of the fence."

"Sure . . . okay . . . ah . . . well, somebody has a little digging problem." Jake's shoulders slumped as he turned and crawled in one of the doghouses.

"*Who* has a digging problem?" Ding looked in the doghouse at Jake.

"Somebody." Jake pouted.

"Tell them!" Ding growled back at the doghouse.

"Okay. I guess *I* have a little digging problem. I start digging and I just can't stop. I start looking for treasure and I just have to keep digging. I can dig all that I want to in here. I have a great spot over there. When it's hot, I just dig it out a little. When it gets uncomfortable, I just dig a little more." Jake's head drooped on the floor of his doghouse.

"Truthfully, he has a *big* digging problem." Ding sighed. "I don't know where the dirt goes. Andy tries to fill the holes back in, and there's never enough dirt."

I tilted my head to one side. "Why are you in here? Do you have a digging problem, too?"

"I'm here to keep him company. When I was young, I used to patrol the place at night. You know—keep coyotes and raccoons and skunks away. But to tell you the truth, it's pretty comfortable to be all cozy in here when the coyotes are howling."

"How did you get here?" I asked the old dog.

"I was pretty young when I got dumped. Lots of places that I went didn't want me.

This place . . . well, I was lucky enough to get to stay. Bethany and Andy hadn't lived here very long. They already had three dogs then."

"Jake, Biff, and Barkie? Right?"

"No." The old dog shook her head, then walked around in a couple of small circles before she lay down in the dust. "Jake's only been here for a couple of years. Biff and Barkie belonged to Andy's mother. She died last year. They used to come visit with her. Then they had to live here. They try to sound grouchy, but they are really okay."

"They seem to be all right," I said with a shrug of my ears. "They just don't know us very well yet."

Spike moved closer to the fence. "What about you, Jake?"

"It's kind of hard to remember. We were out hunting for birds. I had pointed lots of quail, things were going pretty good. I guess I took a wrong turn, but I kept hunting. When I looked up, Robert was gone. I was exhausted when I got here. Andy fed me and Bethany petted me. They made a nice pen for me. Lots of people came and looked at me, but not Robert. So I got to stay!"

Jake stood up in his doghouse, turned around, and flopped back down in the straw and bedding.

"Where are the three dogs that were here when you came, Ding?" I looked at the old dog.

"You're a smart dog. You know what happens when you get old, right? We don't live forever. Just like all living things, new life comes along, and the old have to make room for them. Bethany and Andy have a special place for us when we die, out there under the trees. Some people just dump dead animals. Bethany and Andy bury their pets, then put up rocks and markers so that they will remember the special times we had together." Ding stretched as she got up.

"That's kind of sad," Spike whimpered.

"No, it's really great. None of us can stay forever. It means that we are important enough that they will remember us for a long time after we are gone. I'm glad that they will make a special place for me when I die. I don't want them to be sad. I'm glad that they will remember the good times that we had together." Ding took a mouthful of food before she settled back down in the dirt.

Spike plopped on his rump and his eyebrows kind of scrunched down.

"You trust these people, don't you?"

Ding's tail gave a little wag. "I trust them a lot."

Spike seemed to bristle. "I lived in a junkyard and the people there weren't much fun. As a matter of fact, they were downright mean. Then we were on the road, and that wasn't any fun, either." He rubbed his tongue against the roof of his mouth. "Grasshoppers are crunchy," he mumbled, more to himself than to them, "but they taste yucky."

"Bethany and Andy are okay. You can trust them. They will take care of you. Andy gets a bit upset with her when she tries to take care of too much stuff. She always tries to find a good home for lost pets. If it isn't the right place, she won't let them go. She has a kind heart. This is a good place."

CHAPTER 8

A few mornings later sunlight was already streaming through the trees, when the front door opened wide. Bethany and Andy brought the little dogs out. Spike lay beside me, rolled in a ball in the grass. I flopped to my stomach and perked my ears.

Bethany led Biff out onto the grass and set Barkie down. "Go on. Do your morning doo, doggers." She smiled.

The little dogs stretched and headed for the fence.

Andy sat down on the front steps. Beside him was a flat tray with rows of little plants in it. He and Bethany had been working in her flower garden. He scooted some of the garden tools aside and frowned. "I think Barkie's arthritis is bothering her. Those old legs aren't working like they should."

Bethany walked over to where we had been sleeping. She always rubbed my ears, then my face. Even when she was in a hurry, she'd scratch my back, then fluff my head. The ridge on Spike's back had finally quit standing up every time Bethany and Andy came near.

The little dogs were busy sniffing the grass. I followed Bethany back to the porch. Against the side of the house was a small table with four flowerpots on top. She turned each pot, just a little, so the flowers could get some sunshine, then she sat down beside Andy. I nudged her hand with my nose.

"Didn't get enough of your morning love time?" Bethany laughed, rubbing my face. Then she reached around my neck and snuggled me close.

Andy leaned toward Spike and clapped his hands. "Come on, Tough Guy. Come get your rubdown. You want to be part of this, don't you?" Spike tilted his head to one side and perked his ears. "Come on. You've put this off long enough."

Spike stood as still as he could, then suddenly he raced to the porch. He almost knocked me down as he plopped his front paws on Andy's lap.

"About time you relaxed a little." Andy rubbed the slick fur on Spike's back. Then he scratched behind his ears.

"I have tried to get that dog to let me touch him ever since they got here," Bethany huffed. "Now, here he is practically sitting on your lap. I can't believe it."

"You're a fine-looking dog, Tough Guy!" Andy stroked Spike's back.

"Grrrr," Biff growled. "Get out of our way, you big mutts. We need our time with them." He stood stiff-legged on the edge of the porch.

"Bethany, will you please put them inside? Tough Guy has finally let me get close to him. It's not the best time for those two to get temperamental." Andy snuggled Spike closer.

"Scoot over, Beautiful. Let me get these two out of here." Bethany gave me a quick hug, then scooped Biff and Barkie up off the porch and took them inside. When Bethany came back, she started rubbing my face again. I laid my head in her lap and relaxed. We stayed that way for a long time. I loved the way she stroked and cuddled. I could have stayed with my head in her lap forever. And I would have . . .

Trouble was, Bethany and Andy had a cat!

We had seen the big fuzz ball staring at us from the window a few times. He seemed like a calm cat. He'd just glare at us or the birds who fluttered around the feeder that Bethany kept filled with seeds. Spike watched him, but never acted like he wanted to chase him or anything else for that matter. But this was a little bit different.

Screech, scratch. My ears perked at the sound when something clawed at the screen.

"Are you going to let that cat out?" Andy whispered to Bethany.

Spike didn't move.

Bethany shrugged. "I don't know. These two are being so calm, I hate to spoil the mood. That cat comes out—hard telling what will happen."

"Ah, let him out," Andy urged, pulling Spike

a little closer. "He's a real rugged cat. He won't take anything off these two."

Slow and quiet, Bethany got up and walked to the front door.

"Okay, Deeker, come on out," she said, opening the door just a bit. With her foot, she reached down and scooted a brick into the opening so it wouldn't slam shut.

Tail swishing, the big black cat sauntered onto the porch.

"Calm down, Tough Guy," Andy soothed as he held on to Spike's shoulders. "It's okay."

The hair on my friend's back rose slowly, but he didn't growl or anything.

The black cat looked at Spike. His yellow eyes popped big.

"Phhhhissss!" The black cat arched his back. His tail puffed—tripling in size. Eyes wide, he pressed himself against the wall, almost flattening into the bricks.

"What's the matter with Deeker?" Andy asked, stretching his neck so he could look around at the big cat.

"I have *no* idea," Bethany answered. "He's been watching them from the window. I mean . . . it's not like he didn't know they were here. Maybe he's uncomfortable, since he usually goes out the back door." Her grip relaxed on me when she could tell I wasn't going anywhere.

Suddenly Spike leaped away from Andy.

My heart sank.

This was the "House Cat." If Spike ate him, Andy and Bethany wouldn't like us anymore.

Spike took off.

The cat took off.

I cringed. *Oh, no!*

Then . . .

Mouth gaping wide, I blinked. Then I blinked again.

Spike wasn't going to eat the cat. Spike wasn't even running toward the cat. He took off for the front yard. Only thing, when he leaped from Andy's grasp, he ran smack-dab into the little black tray of plants that sat beside them. Flowers flew all over the place, and the garden tools clattered across the porch. In the blink of an eye, he was gone.

The cat went the same direction. Instead of jumping off the porch like Spike did, he leaped up onto the little table for safety. The table

rocked. The cat rocked. His tail spun in circles a couple of times as the table tilted, then tipped.

There was a loud clatter when the pots crashed to the ground. It made me blink. When I opened my eyes again—the crazy cat was gone!

Andy's mouth fell open as wide as mine was. "What in the world was that all about?"

Bethany blinked a couple of times. Her mouth was open, too. "He must be afraid of Deeker. And Deeker . . . well, the dog must have scared him . . . and . . . and . . . well, they both took off like crazy."

Stepping over the shattered clay pots, she walked to the corner and started calling for Spike. "Come on, Tough Guy. We won't let that cat get you. Come on."

Andy climbed around the porch on all fours and started scooping some of the dirt back into the little black tray. "I thought things were going to be better. That dog finally lets us touch him, and then he goes totally berserk over a cat. Wacky dog." He paused a second, frowned, then smiled. "Maybe *that* should be his name. Wacky Dog." Andy shook his head. When he looked at the place where Spike disappeared around the house, his eyes kind of rolled. "Running from a little old cat . . ." his voice trailed off as he picked up a broom and started sweeping the porch.

"It'll be better when they meet in the backyard," Bethany said, strolling back from the edge of the porch.

I breathed a sigh of relief, now that all the excitement was over. That Spike's one daffy dog, I thought.

"The backyard is Deeker's space," Bethany went on. "He'll take to these guys. I know he will."

She knelt down to help Andy. They swept the dirt and broken pots into a pile. Then they gathered the little flowers and put them back in the dirt they saved in the black tray. When they were finished, they went inside. Andy closed the door behind them.

I didn't like being all alone, so I trotted to the side of the house to see what had happened to my friend. When I got there, I looked all around, but Spike was no place in sight. I finally spotted him, hiding behind a big oak tree, way out beyond the fence.

"What was that about?" I barked. "Everything was calm and you go nuts. What happened?"

Eyes wide, Spike peeked around the tree trunk.

"Is it gone?"

"Is what gone?"

"That big black thing. It had a huge tail and sharp claws. Didn't you see it? It hissed at us. What was it?" Spike was still shaking when he leaned out a bit farther. "I've never seen anything like that. It was scary!"

Once more he ducked back to hide. I blinked. Then I shook my head so hard, the loose skin on my neck flopped.

"You mean you were afraid of that little cat?"

"Cat? Is that what that thing was? It was going to get us." Spike eased from behind the tree once more.

"Get real!" I trotted toward him, trying really hard to keep from laughing my tail off. "It was just a little bitty old house cat. What's to be afraid of?"

Spike wouldn't leave the safety of his tree. I marched right up and looked him square in the eye. "You scared off those coyotes, remember? Coyotes are dangerous. They were going to eat us, but you just strutted up and chased them away. That was a house cat. Dogs chase cats. Cats run from us, *we don't run* from them."

"Are you sure?"

"Trust me on this one, Spike. Don't chase him, because Bethany and Andy like him. But you don't need to be afraid of a cat. Okay?"

"Okay," he answered—only he didn't sound too sure.

I couldn't believe this crazy mutt. I clamped my lips and nose shut so I wouldn't burst out laughing. Once back in the front yard, I finally found the cat. When everything started falling and crashing, I guess he darted back inside the house. We spotted him watching out the window. Wide-eyed and still all fuzzed up, he ducked down when he saw us looking at him.

We didn't see the cat again until we moved to the backyard. A truck full of men drove up the driveway one morning. Spike went crazy. He snarled and growled and barked. He even bit at the wire fence. Andy came out with a blue leash.

"Okay, you two. We can't have this. These guys are going to be here a few days. We can't have any teeth marks in them." I leaned against his leg and wagged my tail.

Andy ignored me and slipped the blue leash around Spike's neck. "Come on, Tough Guy. Let's go inside the small pen at the back of the yard."

I followed them to the back gate. Andy let Jake and Ding into the big backyard and shoved Spike into their pen. I followed my friend inside and Andy closed the gate behind us. For a minute Spike acted almost sheepish. Head bowed and tail tucked, he wandered around and sniffed our new pen. Then he settled down and relaxed a bit.

That was until one of the men came into the backyard and shook hands with Andy.

Spike leaped up and charged the fence. He hit it so hard, I thought he was going to knock a hole in the chain-link. He growled and snarled and threw himself again and again into the wire.

This was weird. Faced with the coyotes, Spike was cool and calm as could be. When the cat came outside, Spike ran to hide. Now . . .

"Spike!" I barked. "What is wrong with you? Why are you acting so crazy?"

"That man is in Andy's yard. He's touching him."

"So?"

"I like Andy. He's nice to me. He pets me and says nice things to me. I don't want that stranger around him. If he hurts my Andy . . . I'm . . . I'm going to . . ."

Again he flung himself against the fence. He snarled and barked and . . . and . . .

This was scary!

CHAPTER 9

Spike didn't calm down until the men finally got into their pickup and drove away. Only then did the hair slowly flatten out on his back. Jake and Ding just sat by our fence and stared at us.

"Hey, dog. You're going to have serious problems if you keep that up. Guarding the yard is one thing, but you're overdoing it, don't you think?" Ding scratched her ear with her hind foot.

"I have to protect Andy. Those people were in his yard. I have to take care of him." The hair on Spike's back came up just a little.

"That guy wasn't going to hurt him. You got

to think about these things. You're going to get in deep trouble, dog!"

The back door opened and Jake and Ding ran to greet Bethany.

"Hey, doggers!" She dropped down to stroke their faces. After a good rub, she walked over to our pen. "What are you two doing?"

Spike jumped around the pen as she opened the gate and walked in. Quickly she petted him, then she caressed my face and scratched my back and neck before she turned back to Spike.

"Hey, Tough Guy. What are we going to do about you? You got a little carried away when those men came to fix the fence. They're working down in the pasture, but they may need to come to the house occasionally. You can't go bonkers every time they show up." Bethany scratched under Spike's chin and brushed at his tail before she stood up. "Be good doggers."

Jake and Ding walked up to the fence as Bethany started out the gate.

"You're being sweet dogs today," she told them. "Not one single hole in the yard."

Bethany rubbed Ding's ears and patted Jake on the head before she walked back to the house. Spike and I stood in the small pen and watched her. Ding strutted up to us and kicked some grass with his hind feet.

"See. Told you so. If you don't behave, you'll never get out of that cage. They may even get rid of you."

"She's right," Jake said. "This is a great place to live. You got to get with the program, Spike, or you'll be out of here." Jake turned back toward the house. Walking in circles, he finally curled up in the grass.

"Sounds like good advice to me." I shook my fur before I settled down in the dust.

"I really don't know what happens." Spike's ears drooped. "I just get real nervous when a stranger shows up."

Comforting him, I kissed him on the cheek with my long tongue. "We haven't even been here long enough to know who the strangers are."

"Yeah, I guess. But sometimes you just can't be too careful." Spike dropped his rear to the ground, closed his eyes, and sniffed the breeze. I settled down for a little dog nap.

* * *

I hadn't been asleep very long when I heard the creak of the back door. Spike and I both stood up and leaned into the fence. The cat sauntered into the backyard, his tail flipping as he walked. I shot a worried glance at Spike.

Spike moved away from the fence. The fur on his back came up slowly as the cat stepped into the yard and moved closer to our pen. Jake and Ding sniffed the cat, then curled up in the sunshine. Then the cat called Deeker headed toward our small enclosure. I perked my ears as he approached. I heard a faint growl as Spike moved behind me.

"Hey, dog! What's the matter with your friend? I'm not here to cause any trouble. I think we must have gotten off on the wrong paw."

"I'm not sure what happened the other day." Spike stood right behind me, shaking just a little.

"What's going on, dog? I'm not here to hurt you. I want to be friends. This is a super place to live. You don't need to be scared of me. I won't bother you *if* you won't bother me.

Okay?" The cat rubbed against the wire cage.

"Hey, I . . . I don't have a problem with that." Spike's voice shook just a little.

"Good deal. I stay in the house most of the time, so you won't even have to see me. When I come out, I stay pretty close to the backyard. Coyotes, you know. I can usually avoid them, but I don't want to be surprised by one." Deeker stretched out his front paws, then dropped down to the ground. He started washing his legs with his pink tongue.

"I'm . . . I'm really not afraid of you. You just sort of . . . ah . . . startled me. I never met a cat before." Sniffing, Spike moved closer to the fence.

"Most of us are okay. It never hurts to be careful. There are some pretty big cats out there. Usually house cats like me just need a little bit of outdoor time." The cat jumped up when the back door opened.

"Deeker? Deeker? Where are you, cat? Come on back in here," Andy's voice called.

"Got to go. I don't always mind when I get called. You know—I have to remind them who's really boss around here, sometimes—

but I haven't eaten yet. Can't miss a meal! See you later." The cat bounded off toward the house.

Spike and I had lots of good days when Andy started letting us out for morning runs. First thing in the day, he would let Jake, Ding, Spike, and me loose for a short sprint. Ding didn't sprint. She kind of hobbled to the end of the driveway, stretched, and waddled back to the yard. Jake usually ran big circles around her, then made a couple of loops around the front yard. Spike and I explored the trees and brush near the house. We stayed close enough to hear Andy when he called us back into the yard.

This morning we hadn't been out very long when a big delivery truck roared up the driveway. Spike's fur ruffled to a sharp ridge on his back. Andy started calling us to come back in. A low growl came from my friend's throat as Andy put a rope around his neck.

"Calm down, Spike. You'll get us put back in the little pen," I warned him.

"Come on, Tough Guy. He isn't going to

hurt you." Andy pulled Spike back into the yard. Jake and I followed them. Ding sat in the grass near the fence and barked at the big truck.

It was more than Spike could take. He barked and growled at the man who stepped out.

"He's a rowdy one." The man strolled up to Andy.

"He really is a pretty sweet dog. You're right though, I don't trust him with people around." Andy took a package from the man.

Spike kept barking, but he didn't bite at the fence like he did the last time.

"Calm down, Spike." My eyes narrowed when I stared at him. "Andy has control of this."

As the big truck drove away, Andy put the box down and came over to us.

"Look, Tough Guy. I know you are trying to take care of things, but sometimes you get a little carried away. I'll let you know if we need any help, okay?" Andy ruffled Spike's fur and petted my head before he walked off.

After that Spike barked and barked to let

Andy know when someone was coming. As soon as Andy came out of the house, Spike stood at attention, but he didn't bark or threaten anyone.

The next time the deliveryman came, Spike even walked up to the fence and licked the guy's hand.

Things were pretty good after that. We had time out of the yard in the morning. We had romp time with Jake in the backyard. Spike would chase him around and I would hide and jump out at him. Then Spike would chase me and Jake would hide and jump out. Mostly, Ding would sit in the sun and watch. One evening Andy and Bethany even had people come over for dinner. They cooked out and we all got along. Spike didn't bark once while they were in the backyard. He even started acting like he didn't know they were there.

It was pretty calm for several days. That was until the black truck drove up.

At first I couldn't figure it out. Spike stood staring at the road as the vehicle rumbled and puttered toward the house. Suddenly that ridge of fur stood straight up on his back and neck. His ears flattened and he started barking. Well . . . it was more like roaring. It was the most ferocious sound I had *ever* heard.

Spike snapped and snarled at the fence as two men stepped away from the truck.

"There's that rotten mutt. I knew we would find him, sooner or later." My tail drooped when I recognized that voice.

Roy and Zack stomped up to the fence. Spike bared his teeth and snarled.

"Well, if it isn't my little junkyard friend. Where have you been, you mangy mongrel? Did you think you could get away from me?" Roy kicked at the fence.

"Hey, Spike. Calm down," I warned. "He wants you to be mean. Cool it or he'll try to take you back to the junkyard. You don't want that, do you?"

"Hey, Zack. This guy is getting better. I did a good job of training him, don't you think?"

"Yeah, but we'd better get out of here." Zack turned away from the fence.

"We'll be back, Mutt! The sheriff can take care of this. I'll bet these people stole our watchdog." Roy's chuckle was sinister and

mean as he climbed into the truck.

Tires squealing, they backed the truck out of the driveway. Dirt flew when they peeled away.

Spike kept barking at the truck. From his tone, I could tell he would tear the tires off the thing if he ever got the chance.

"Hey, what's going on out here?" Andy stepped out the back door. A towel was wrapped around his waist.

Spike ran over to him and licked his hand. He started jumping up and down. His dirty feet left brown paw prints on Andy's towel.

"What's this about? What's all the racket?" Andy lifted Spike's paws off him and then crouched down to Spike's level. "What's the matter with my little Tough Guy?"

"I've got to get out of here. Roy's going to get me," Spike whined.

"You're okay. Was there something that scared you? I heard you barking, but I was in the shower and couldn't get out here." Andy stood up and walked to the fence.

"It's Roy. He's coming after me." Spike started growling at the fence.

"I don't see anything. Must have been a coyote or something." Andy looked at the little pen in the back. Ding and Jake were huddled against the fence.

"What's the matter with you two?" Andy called.

Tails tucked they ran to him.

"What's going on out here, anyway? I'll get some clothes on and check around the fence." Andy petted me on the back, then rubbed Jake and Ding's ears before he disappeared into the house.

"I have to find a way to escape. Roy will be back. He'll really be mean when he gets me to the junkyard. You've got to help me. He may even take you." Spike shook all over.

"Easy, Spike. Easy. Andy will take care of everything. You've got to trust him." I sat on my haunches staring at my friend. I had never seen him so scared or worried.

"It's pretty hard to trust anyone. People are so difficult. Maybe Andy called Roy. They already have plenty of dogs. I'm just another mouth to feed." Spike's tail tucked under his tummy as he stood, staring at the gate.

"Where did you come up with that one?

Andy and Bethany have *never* been mean to us. What are you talking about?" I looked at Spike's face. It was tight and mean looking.

"People." Spike snorted. (Only his snort sounded more like a whimper.) "You just can't trust anybody."

"Maybe you'd better try. These people are good to us." I licked Spike's face.

"I don't know, Freddie. If I have to go back to the junkyard . . . if they take me . . . It's awful there." Spike finally stretched out. His head still quivered as he pointed to the road.

I guess what happened next was my fault.

We were talking so intensely that we didn't hear Andy when he came back outside. Fact was, I only noticed him from the corner of one eye, when he leaned down to pet Spike. I guess Roy was the only thing on Spike's mind—that and his fear—no, terror—at the thought of having to go back to the junkyard.

Andy took one more step. His weight was on his heel. But when he leaned forward to pet Spike . . . well . . . the front of his foot was right over Spike's tail. I didn't even have time to bark a warning.

Spike's eyes flashed wide as he yelped in pain, sprang to his feet, and whirled around.

My heart sank clear down into my belly when I saw his sharp fangs flash.

Andy yelled.

It was too late!

"Let go of him, Spike," I yelped.

Instantly Spike's jaws sprang open. "Oh, no! I've done it now!"

Tail tucked so far under him that it looked like part of his stomach, Spike scooted to the fence. He looked like he'd been beaten with a club or something, the way he cowered against the chain link with his head bowed so low it almost touched the ground.

"What in the world is wrong with you, dog?" Andy hopped around, rubbing at his leg. "I was just going to pet you. Are you hurt?"

CHAPTER 10

Spike ran to the little pen at the end of the yard. He scooted into the doghouse and shoved himself all the way to the back.

"What's wrong with that dog?" I followed Andy as he walked to where Spike was hiding. He leaned over and rubbed his leg before he looked in. "Hey, buddy. What's going on with you?"

Andy and I peered into the dark opening.

"I messed up—big time." Spike whimpered. "I'm so ashamed. I love Andy. I didn't mean to bite him. I'd never . . ." He broke off, sniffling.

"Hey, Tough Guy. I didn't mean to step on your tail. Are you okay? Come on out and let me look at it." Andy squatted in front of the doghouse. "Silly dog. Come out and let me look you over. Are you really hurt?"

Shouldering my way past Andy, I stuck my head inside. "Spike, you better let him look at you. Are you hurt really bad?"

"Get back. Leave me alone, Freddie. I'm bad news. I bit Andy. He'll get rid of me for sure. And if you're around, he'll dump you, too!" Spike flattened himself against the back of the doghouse.

Spike's words sent a chill racing up my back. *"He'll dump you, too!"*

The words seemed to echo inside of my head. Slowly, one step at a time, I backed away from my friend.

I had been dumped once. I had no idea why— no clue as to what I did to be driven in the car . . . away from my boy . . . and left alone in the rain. I liked people. I needed them. Andy and Bethany were good to me. They petted me and loved me. I couldn't bear the thought of losing that.

Tail tucked between my legs, I slinked to the far side of the yard.

Andy reached in to get Spike. "Come on,

Tough Guy. Let's see if you're hurt."

Spike stuck all four legs out and stiffened his whole body to keep Andy from pulling him out of the small enclosure.

"Come on, dog. I'm going to win this one. You might as well make it easy. I know where the leash is and you are coming out of there." Andy grabbed the back of Spike's neck.

Very slowly, Spike relaxed as Andy dragged him from his house. He looked him over—especially his tail—petted him a bit, then let him go. As soon as he did, Spike shot back into the shadows of the doghouse.

"I didn't mean to step on your tail," Andy said again. "It couldn't have hurt that bad. Something else must be going on. Did something scare you before I came out here? I'll go have a look around." Andy walked out of the gate.

As soon as he was gone, Jake and Ding trotted to the doghouse.

"What's going on?" Ding asked, leaning in to smell Spike.

"It was Roy. He's from the junkyard, and he'll be coming back for me. Andy doesn't understand. He doesn't know Roy."

Even from my hiding place at the far side of the yard, I could understand them.

"Andy will do everything he can to take care of you," Jake assured him. "If Roy comes back, Andy will figure out what's going on. You're safe. He will protect you. He protects all of us."

"But . . . but I bit Andy." Spike sniffed.

Ding shrugged her ears. "It was an accident. You didn't mean to. Andy knows that. He and Bethany are good people."

"You guys are safe," Andy promised when he came through the gate. "Didn't see a thing. Not even a track. You're okay. I've got to get out of here. Bethany will be back before lunch. I'll leave her a note so that she will know that you are jittery about something. Okay, guys?"

The rest of the day I kept an eye on Spike, but I didn't get near him. It wasn't until Bethany got back that he started acting normal again. By evening he was hopping around like nothing had happened. I still kept my distance. I never thought I could love someone as much as I did my boy. But Andy and Bethany were special. For people—they were wonderful. If they sent Spike away for biting Andy . . . If they dumped me, too . . . Just the thought of losing them . . . the thought of being dumped . . . again . . .

The next morning I woke with a start. I heaved a sigh of relief when I realized I was still in the yard. After I stretched, did my morning business, and kicked the grass, I glanced at the doghouse. Spike wasn't in his usual spot. He must have taken off in the night. I yelped for Jake and Ding. Ding slowly pulled herself out of one of the doghouses.

"What's wrong?" Jake came running from the corner of the yard.

"Where's Spike? Did he get out?" I growled. "Did he run away?"

"No, he's in the doghouse out in that pen. He crawled in there in the middle of the night." Jake turned and sniffed the breeze.

Ding waddled up to us. "What's with you two, anyhow?"

"What do you mean?" I cocked an ear.

"You two stick to each other like pancakes

and syrup stick to the roof of my mouth."

My other ear raised. "Pancakes and syrup? What's that?"

Jake wagged his tail. "You'll see. Every time Bethany fixes pancakes, she always makes extra for us. They're really sweet and good and—"

"Knock it off with the pancakes," Ding growled. "I'm talking to Freddie." She glared at me. "You and Spike are good friends. But for a whole day and night, you haven't even been near each other. What's going on between you and Spike?"

I couldn't look at her. I turned to sniff at the fence.

"Nothing's going on. What do you mean?"

"Something's wrong." Ding followed me and nudged me with her snout. "Did you two have a fight or something?"

I curled my tail out of the way and plopped down on my rump. For a long time I couldn't look at her. Finally I took a deep breath.

"He bit Andy. He didn't mean to. But he did. And . . . and if Andy sends him away, he'll send me away, too. I've been dumped before. My boy loved me. I had a nice, safe yard to live in.

Then . . . DUMPED! Nobody loved me. It hurt so bad and . . . if it happens again . . ."

All the fear and hurt and sadness just poured out of me. My story tumbled and rushed like water dashing down a stream, and I couldn't stop it until I had told Ding everything.

She sat next to me all the time I talked. She even leaned her head against my shoulder. When I finished, she kissed me gently on the cheek with her long tongue.

"Except for Biff and Barkie, we're all strays," she said. "Jake and me, the dogs who came before us, the dogs who will come after you— all dumped. That's how we came to live with Andy and Bethany. None of us can forget how it feels, not to be needed or loved, but—"

"Yeah, me, too," Jake interrupted.

Ding shot him a stern look.

"But," she repeated, turning to me. "But you and Spike are friends."

That was all she said. The look in her eye left a chill inside me. It almost made me feel as cold and lonely and empty as I did when I found myself deserted at that park. I didn't like it. For that matter . . . I didn't like me too much, either.

127

* * *

About thirty minutes later Andy came out of the house. He marched straight to the doghouse and peeked in at Spike.

"Hey, dog. Rise and shine."

Spike jumped up and leaped through the doorway. He nearly knocked Andy over, licking and jumping up on him.

"Calm down, Tough Guy. You need to get some of that extra energy run off. Let's go for a jog." Andy opened the back gate and let us all out for our morning romp.

We had fun checking out all the smells that might have been left by critters which had come in the night. We also chased mice that rustled in the grass. Spike, Jake, and I followed trails in the pasture. Ding waddled along behind, stopping now and then to sniff at some really good odors. When we got back to the house, Andy had just closed us in the backyard when a car drove up the driveway.

Spike ran for the doghouse as Jake, Ding, and I started barking at the sound that was coming closer.

Andy stood at the gate. When the car

stopped in the driveway, he walked out and closed the gate behind him. A man in a uniform stepped out.

"Yes, sir. What can I do for you?" Andy stood at the man's car door.

"I'm Nathan Jones with the Sheriff's Department. We had a complaint come in that you had a stolen dog. It's a trained guard dog." The man looked toward us.

"I don't think we have anyone's trained dog. These dogs are all strays that someone has dumped. You're welcome to look at them." Andy stepped back so that the sheriff man could see us.

I barked a bit more, but Ding howled like she was hearing coyotes or something. Jake's tail wagged. Spike was gone!

"People from town are always letting their dogs loose out here. My wife's real bad about adopting strays. But I don't think anyone would want these guys for a guard dog." Andy reached through the links of the fence to touch my face.

"Are these all you have?"

"No, we have Tough Guy somewhere. He's really just a sweet little dog, though." Holding his hands above his eyes to shield them from the noon sun, Andy scanned the yard. "Tough Guy. Come here, pup."

We all looked around for Spike. He was crouched in the back of the doghouse.

"Let me get him. He couldn't possibly be the one you're looking for." Andy went in the house and came back with a blue leash. He walked to the doghouse, bent over, and looped the rope around Spike's neck. Reluctantly the dog came out.

When they came through the gate, Andy dropped down and started petting him. The sheriff reached over and rubbed Spike's head.

"I don't think any of these could be the one they are looking for. You haven't had any others around here lately have you?" The sheriff man rubbed Spike's face, one last time, and got up.

"We haven't seen one lately. These last two have only been here a few weeks. Dogs get dumped out here all the time. I don't understand what people are thinking. Dogs that count on people for their food can't take care of themselves out in the country. The pound at least tries to find homes for them." Andy took the leash off Spike before he let him back in the yard.

"I'll have to check back with the office. I'm pretty sure this is the address they gave me, but it can't be any of these dogs. They're too sweet and gentle. I appreciate your time. Sorry to have bothered you."

"No problem. Hope you find your stolen dog." Andy closed the gate. We all got a good petting before he went back in the house. That was a close call, I thought with a sigh of relief. Maybe it's over. Maybe we're finally safe.

Jake, Ding, Spike, and I were having a little romp when the black truck drove up the driveway. The sheriff man's car was behind it. Jake and Ding ran to bark at the fence. Trembling, Spike shot into the doghouse in the far pen.

I . . . well, all I could do was stand in the middle of the yard. They had come to take Spike back to the junkyard. If I was with him, they'd take me, too.

Then . . . a chill ran up my spine when I remembered the look in Ding's eyes and her words.

"*Spike is your friend.*"

CHAPTER 11

Racing at full speed, I dived through the door of the doghouse. The wooden floor was slicker than I thought. I tried to stop, but I ended up slamming into Spike, who was huddled against the far wall.

There was a little *whoompf* sound. I guess I sort of knocked the air out of him. I struggled to get off, and he struggled to get up.

"Beat it," he whimpered. "Save yourself. They'll take you, too. Run!"

"Shut up and listen to me," I snarled. "Do exactly what I tell you. No matter what happens, don't bark or growl. Just look as sweet as you can."

When Andy came outside, Jake and Ding stopped barking. "What's going on out here?" He blinked when he saw the sheriff's car.

"We want our dog back," Roy called from outside the gate. "And we want to be paid for the time you've had him. We could have been robbed while Spike was gone. You owe us money." Roy gawked around, outside the wire, looking for Spike.

"What are you talking about? I don't have your dog." Andy closed the gate behind him and walked to the sheriff man.

"I'm sorry, sir. Mr. Ferguson here says that you do have his dog."

"Which one of them do you think it is?" Andy rested his elbows on the fence and nodded toward the yard. I stood in the doorway of the doghouse, between Roy and the shadows where my friend hid.

"I've seen that one before." Roy pointed at me. "But that's not Spike. My dog's mean. He's a trained guard dog. We've missed that dog's services while you had him. We want him back, and we want to be paid for the time he's been gone. Where are you hiding him?"

"Tough Guy is probably in the doghouse, over there. But I don't think he's the one you're looking for. He's a sweet dog. He's even afraid of our cat."

"Well, let me look at him." Roy's voice was gruff and nasty. "Spike ain't sweet. He's tough. If he ain't still that way, you must have done something to him. We had that dog trained."

"Just a minute, sir," the sheriff man interrupted. "It's not any of these? Is that correct?"

"Nah," Roy said, turning back to the sheriff man.

"Are you positive?"

Roy's lip curled up on one side. "I told you, he ain't out here. This guy must have our dog hidden somewhere. I saw him here the other day."

"When were you here before?" Andy asked the man.

"We were out looking for Spike day before yesterday. The sheriff told us we had to wait until a deputy could come, 'fore we could get him. Now give me my dog." The man started to pull the latch up on the gate.

"Would you please let him see that other

dog," the sheriff man said, stopping Roy from opening the latch. Roy's lip curled again when he looked down. He yanked his hand from the sheriff man's grasp.

"I'll get him." Andy started for the doghouse where Spike was huddled behind me. When he got to our pen, he started to kneel down and reach past me.

I took a deep breath, made the hair bristle to a sharp ridge down my back, and . . .

Let out the loudest, deepest roar I'd ever barked in my whole entire life.

Andy's eyes flashed wide. He yanked his hand back.

"What's gotten into you?" he asked me.

Just the sound of his voice made my tail want to wag. I wouldn't let it. Instead, I squinted my eyes, gritted my teeth, and roared again.

Andy took a step back. Spike growled.

"Don't you hurt Andy. I love him. I never meant to bite him. When I did, I made a promise to myself that I'd never bite anyone or anything, ever again. But so help me . . . if you hurt Andy . . ."

"I'm not going to hurt Andy," I whispered over my shoulder. "Just do what I told you. Don't bark. Don't growl. Don't even show your teeth."

"Not even at Roy?"

"Especially not at Roy!"

Andy shook his head and moved toward our doghouse again. I snarled and barked and snapped. Head tilted far to one side, he looked at me a moment.

"What is wrong with you? You've never acted like this." Andy stomped his foot, snapped his fingers, and pointed to the ground beside him. "You get out here! RIGHT NOW!"

Tail tucked, I slipped through the doorway and went to stand where he pointed. I leaned against his leg and rubbed his knee with my cheek.

"That's the weirdest thing . . ." I heard him say, more to himself than to me.

Spike whimpered softly as Andy reached in the doghouse. "Come on, Tough Guy. You can't be the one these guys are looking for."

Slowly Andy pulled him out. Tail tucked and ears drooped, Spike's brown eyes were wide open.

"Is *this* the mean, vicious guard dog that you've been looking for?" I heard the sheriff ask.

"They must have done something to him. They've probably been hitting him or something. They are going to owe us big time." Roy kicked at the fence when Andy dragged Spike closer.

"Sheriff Jones, I don't think this could be his dog. He's shaking like a leaf. If this man actually had him, he must have been treating him pretty rough." Andy rubbed Spike's ears. Spike's tail wagged just a little.

"Just give me my dog!" Roy's ugly face looked really mean when he started to open the gate once more.

"Just a minute, Mr. Ferguson. I think there's something really wrong here. When I came out this morning, that dog was happy and jumping around. The big fluffy one"—he nodded toward me—"well, he was sweet as could be. Now that you're here, he's like a different dog. The one you claim is your guard dog acts like he's scared of *you*." The sheriff man walked into the yard and squatted down to pet Spike.

Jake, Ding, and I all pushed in close to them. I held my breath, hoping Spike wouldn't growl or bite at the sheriff man. He didn't.

"That's a good dog. You aren't any kind of guard dog, are you, pup?" The sheriff man looked Spike over, then let go of him and petted each of us. As soon as he was free, Spike ran to the safety of the doghouse.

"That's my dog and I'm going to have him. There's laws, you know." Roy puffed out his chest.

"Well, sir, if this is your dog, how did you train him?" Andy asked, staring the ugly man square in the eye. "Did you poke him and punch him? Is that why he's acting like this?"

"We didn't hurt him. We just did what we had to do to make him a good watchdog."

Zack's elbow flew out and jabbed Roy in the ribs. Roy sneered at him and rubbed his side.

"Ouch! What's that about?"

Before Zack could answer, the sheriff man leaned his arms on the fence and smiled at Roy.

"Well, that's strange. In the report you gave us, you said that you'd paid five hundred dollars to get this dog professionally trained. Now you're saying that you trained him. Is that right?"

"No . . . no. We paid to have him . . . uh . . . uh . . . trained," Roy stammered. "I'm talking about the follow-up stuff that they had us do. The trainer told us to do. Yeah, that's what I meant."

"I know quite a few dog trainers." Andy stood beside the sheriff man. His eyes tightened when he looked at Roy. "Who did you use?"

"Uh . . . I don't remember his name. Smith or something like that." Roy stepped back a little.

"If I had paid someone five hundred dollars, I would know his name for sure. You got a receipt or canceled check for that training?" The sheriff man pulled out a writing pad from his pocket.

The sound of another car came to my ears. I glanced up and saw Bethany pull into the driveway. There was a worried look on her face when she stepped out and came toward the backyard.

"I've had enough of this foolishness," Roy grumped. "We come to fetch our dog back to the dump. All you're supposed to do, Mr. Cop Man, is just see that we get it done and stay out of our way. Come on, Zack. Help me get Spike."

Roy flung the gate open and marched toward the doghouse.

Jake's tail stopped wagging. The hair on Ding's back bristled. I growled.

"What's going on?" Bethany called. Now she was jogging toward us instead of just walking. "Did something happen?"

No one answered her.

"Come here, Spikey Boy. Come on out." Zack looked into the doghouse.

"Get that mangy dog out of there." Roy kicked at the house. When Spike didn't move, he kicked at it again. "Dump it over, Zack. We'll get him, one way or the other."

"I think you boys better back off!" the sheriff man yelled.

Zack picked up the back side of the doghouse, and Spike slid toward the opening. I could hear his feet, frantically scraping on the wood floor. Roy grabbed Spike's leg and finished dragging him out.

"You'd better get over here, or I'll break your leg off, you mangy dog!" the man roared. He raised his fist and glared at Spike.

"Quit yelling at him." Bethany rushed up. "You're scaring the dogs." When her eyes saw his angry fist raised, she grabbed his arm. "Don't! Please don't hit him."

Roy pushed Bethany!

She staggered back. Slipped. And went *kerplop*, right on her bottom.

That was too much!

"Grrrr. Get away from Bethany!" I snapped. Jake and Ding were right behind me. I grabbed hold of Roy's pant leg, snarling and shaking my head so hard I almost knocked myself down.

Roy screamed.

"Get that dog off me. He bit me." Roy slapped me upside the head. The instant I let go, he sprinted for the gate. Zack was hot on his heels as Ding and Jake growled and snapped at them. Andy helped Bethany up off of the ground and dusted her bottom.

"Are you okay, hon?"

"I'm fine." She smiled.

Once safe outside the backyard, with the gate latched, Roy grabbed his leg and started hopping around. As soon as they closed the gate, Jake, Ding, and I started leaping and snarling and snapping at the fence. Spike stood by his overturned doghouse and wagged his tail. The sheriff man stood beside Andy and Bethany.

"Are you all right, ma'am?"

"I'm fine." She smiled again. "Just lost my balance. I'm not hurt."

He nodded, reached down, and gave Spike a friendly pat on the head, then marched to the fence. Roy was still hopping around, holding one leg up in the air.

"I'm going to sue. That dog tried to tear my leg off. I'll probably never be able to walk again. I'm going to sue! Let's go, Zack. Forget that mangy dog. I'm going to get a lawyer. That crazy white dog bit me!" Roy yelled.

Smiling, the sheriff man leaned over the fence. "Would you please pull up your pant leg, sir. I need to see the wound."

Roy stopped hopping around and put both feet on the ground.

"It's bad. It's real bad. I'll probably have to go to the hospital."

"Let me see it, sir," the sheriff man repeated his order.

Roy sneered at him. "No."

"Well, then, hop in my car and I'll drive you to the emergency room."

"No way."

The sheriff man only smiled and pulled the note pad from his pocket.

"Guess I'll need to add that to my report, too." He talked to himself as he wrote on his little pad. "Victim refused to show the injury and refused transportation to seek medical treatment." He looked up and his smile got even bigger. "Let's see . . . what else do I need to put in here. Oh, yeah. Trespassing. You entered the yard illegally and without permission. Destruction of private property. Assault and battery—"

"Assault and battery?" Roy yelped. "No such thing!"

The sheriff man's eyebrows arched. "You attacked the lady over there and knocked her down. I'm a witness."

"She grabbed my arm . . . and . . . and . . ."

"I saw the whole thing." The sheriff man grinned. Then his eyes narrowed as he glared at Roy. "She never touched you!"

"But . . . but . . ." Roy stammered. Reluctantly he reached down and pulled his pant leg up. There wasn't a mark on him.

"That dog didn't even touch you. Go on and leave these nice folks alone," the sheriff man said.

"But look what he did to my pants. First they ruin our guard dog, then they sic that vicious mutt on me. At least they ought to pay for my pants. The leg's all shredded up and . . ."

Zack grabbed Roy's arm and pulled him toward the black truck.

"There was no damage to your person," the sheriff man called after them. "As far as these people stealing your dog . . . I know these people . . . they wouldn't steal your dog. You may have a case if you can prove ownership and a receipt for training a dog. My hunch is that you don't have receipts. Any training your dog ever got came from being knocked around and beaten. Probably need to add animal abuse to this record. There *is* a law against that." The sheriff man stood straight and tall.

"We'll see," Roy remarked over his shoulder.

"My advice to you, sir, is to leave and never come back." The sheriff man *was not* smiling anymore. "This report will be kept in the file. If any of these animals turn up missing or hurt or sick, I'll personally come out to your junkyard and drag you in. Fact is, if these nice people so much as tell me they see your pickup driving down their road—I'm coming after you. Got it?"

Roy didn't answer. He did nod his head, though.

"Ah, come on, Zack. Let's get out of here." He growled, kind of leaning to the side to see past us and look at Spike. "That dog ain't no use to us, anyhow. Never was worth shooting. We'll just get us a better dog."

Roy stepped into the truck and slammed the door. Zack hurried around to get in on his side. Roy took off before he got there. Zack had to jump, open the door, and swing himself in as the truck was moving. Dirt and rocks flew everywhere as the truck roared away.

"Sorry, folks. Everyone in the sheriff's department—police department, too, for that matter—we all know Roy Ferguson. He's about as worthless as they come. Always threatening to sue someone or trying to get money out of them. But he did file a report, and we had to respond to it." The sheriff man walked back to the yard. "He won't bother you again. I'd bet money on it."

"We appreciate all of your help." Andy reached over the fence and shook his hand. "We certainly wouldn't steal anyone's dog!"

Jake, Ding, Spike, and I all ran to put our front paws on the fence. We licked his hand and thanked him, too.

"Good dogs you got." The young man smiled. "They're pretty good judges of character." He ruffled the hair on my head. "This one was going to tear Roy up." I licked his hand again.

With a laugh, he strolled back toward his car.

"Thanks again, Mr. Jones," Andy and Bethany both called as they waved at him.

When things calmed down, Bethany went

inside and fixed us all a special treat. Even Biff and Barkie got pancakes and syrup.

Ding was right. The stuff was yummy, but it did stick to the roof of my mouth.

"I can't believe that big white fluffy dog," Bethany said as she and Andy watched us eat. "He's always been the sweetest thing. Never even growls at the other dogs. I just couldn't believe he was going to tear that guy up."

"Well"—Andy shrugged—"when that man pushed you down, tearing him up was the same thought that crossed my mind. Your white dog just beat me to it."

"Guess we need to keep him around. He's a pretty good watchdog." Bethany petted my head.

Spike trotted up and Andy scratched behind his ears. Tail wagging so fast and hard that it stirred the air, he smiled at me.

"Thanks for helping me, Freddie," he yapped. "You're the best friend a dog could ever have. I love you."

It was good to have a home. Good to feel needed. Good to be loved.

ABOUT THE AUTHORS

Carol Wallace and Bill Wallace have always had lots of pets. Most are "strays" that they have taken in. And most—if not all—became characters in their books.

Mush (who goes by Freddie in this story, but used the name Snow in Bub Moose) is sweet—most of the time; clumsy—some of the time; and so lovable that she wormed her way into their hearts from the very first day she appeared at their home. She's lovable until . . . she finds something stinky to roll in.

April (Spike in the story) is also lovable—with family and friends. When someone unknown shows up . . . LOOK OUT! Just like the other five dogs in the family, she can be the meanest hound around.

Carol Wallace is the wife of award-winning author Bill Wallace. The couple resides in Chickasha, Oklahoma. Carol was an elementary school teacher. Both Bill and Carol hold master's degrees in elementary education from Southwestern Oklahoma State University.

The BILL WALLACE Collection

THE BACKWARD BIRD DOG

by BILL WALLACE

ILLUSTRATED by DAVID SLONIM

To J.C., Carol, and Justin

Chapter 1

Old Blue howled at night.

It was a mournful sound. Soft and low, it crept through the darkness of our kennel that warm summer evening like a snake. The sadness of its cold hard coils wrapped around me, cutting off all the love and comfort that was so near.

I pressed my ears flat against my head, trying to shut out his cry. Still it got through. It made my insides feel as cold and lonely as he was. It hurt.

I shivered and raised my head. Mother was right beside me. I pushed closer to her, hoping her warmth would chase away the chills and the scaries.

"Why does Old Blue cry like that?" I asked.

"He's sad," she answered.

"Why is he sad?"

"He has no nose and he has no My."

I cocked an ear and tilted my head to the side. "What happened to his nose? Did he get it bit off in a fight?"

Mother's tail thumped against the floor. "He really does have a nose," she laughed. "Only it doesn't work. He can't smell quail with it."

"Quail?"

"Yes," she answered. "You see, we're bird dogs. We find quail for our Mys. When we find them, we point at them so our Mys can shoot them. That makes them happy and proud. Old Blue has a nose, but he can't find quail. A bird dog must have a good nose to make our My happy."

"What's a My?"

"A My is a People. Not just any People," she explained. "It's a very special People you love and who loves you."

"What's love?"

Mother took a deep breath. I could feel her sides heave in and out against my cheek. "Love is sort of a thing. Well, no . . . it's more of a feeling . . . it's . . . it's . . . well, love is really hard to explain."

"Please try, Mother," I urged with a shove of my nose. "Please. I really want to know."

Her ears flopped when she shook her head. "I can't. But when you love or when someone loves you . . . well, you just know."

"Will I have a My?"

"Someday."

"And I'll just know, right?"

"You'll know. Now go to sleep before you wake your brothers and sisters."

I lay my head on my paws and closed my eyes. Old Blue howled again. My eye popped open. I crawled over Mother's paw and scooted right up against her cheek. I got so close that my eyeball almost touched hers.

"If I have a nose that doesn't work . . . if I don't have a My . . . will I howl at night, like Old Blue? Will I make his sad, scary sound?"

The big brown eye that stared at me blinked. Mother glanced away for just an instant, then the big brown eye smiled down at me.

"You're such a worrywart."

"What's a worrywart?"

"A puppy who asks dumb questions and keeps his mother awake all night." She winked. "Now, hush and go to sleep. You're going to be just fine."

With that, Mother began to kiss me. Her tongue wrapped about me like a warm blanket. It chased away the scary sadness of Old Blue's howl. It made me feel safe.

If Mother said I was going to be just fine . . . well, that was good enough for me. That's because mothers are about the wisest and bestest

3

things in the whole entire world. Safe and warm, I closed my eyes.

Early the next morning, Roberto and Mr. Tommy opened the top of our bedroom. Mr. Tommy lifted Mother out and closed the roof. My brothers and sisters and I waddled through the opening into the wire pen. Our pen was high up off the ground. But even though our feet slipped through the wire floor all the time, we didn't worry about falling. That was because the openings in the wire were too small for us to fall all the way to the ground. We watched Mother run all around the big yard. She sniffed here and there and used the bathroom, then sniffed some more places. Finally, Mr. Tommy called to her and she came back. Roberto lifted her into the wooden part of our pen and closed the roof. We all scrambled inside with Mama to lie on the hay and get breakfast.

We'd just finished eating when this machine monster came into the Big Yard and stopped by the People house. A man People and a woman People got out. Mr. Tommy went to greet them and they spent a long time making mouth noises. Then the Peoples followed Mr. Tommy all around our kennel. They looked at each dog and made mouth noises. All the dogs wagged their tails and barked and spun around and jumped with their front paws on the chain-link fence.

When they came to Old Blue's pen, he just lay there and looked at them.

The man People and Mr. Tommy spent a long time in front of Big Mike's pen. But it wasn't long before the woman People came over to where we were. My brothers and sisters and I always got excited when a People came by to look at us. Nobody really understood why. I mean, they *are* kind of ugly creatures. Still, there's just something about them that made us all wiggly inside.

Tina was the first to greet her. Tina always was better about walking on the wire than the rest of us. She wagged her tail and stuck her nose through the pen. The woman People rubbed her, then reached in to scratch behind Tina's ears. By then, Ben was there. He shoved Tina out of the way so he could get touched by the woman People, too. I was hot on Ben's heels, but my paw slipped through one of the holes in the wire and I fell. I bumped my chin so hard that it crossed my eyes. It didn't take me long to get up, but it was long enough that Pat and the rest of my brothers and sisters raced past me and got to the edge of the pen first.

The woman People had a soft, pretty voice. She laughed and smiled and petted each of my brothers and sisters. I shoved Pat out of the way with my nose and shoulder. She didn't pet me, though. Instead, she bent way down and looked me square in the eye.

5

"Bill." She made a mouth noise that was so loud it made me blink. "Come over here and look at this little fella."

I took a step back and my hind foot fell through the wire. Ben shoved in front of me. The woman People didn't pet him. She didn't even look at him. Her eyes were still on me.

"See you found the puppies," Mr. Tommy said.

The woman People didn't mouth talk to him. Instead, she kept looking at me. She leaned a bit to the side so the man People could stand next to her.

"Looks a lot like old Slim, doesn't he?" Her voice was very soft, almost sad.

The man People frowned at me. Then he smiled like the woman People did.

"Sure does."

"He's got blue eyes." She reached to pet me as I wedged my way between Ben and Sassy. "Never saw a dog with blue eyes."

"I never noticed that," Mr. Tommy admitted. "He sure does. They'll change, though. As he gets older, they'll turn to what we call deer eyes—sort of a soft brown. It is kind of unusual, though."

I couldn't quite understand all their People noises, but I could tell they were talking about me. I could tell by the way all their eyes were on me. The woman People reached past my brothers and sisters to pet me. Even when Sassy and Pat tried to knock me out of the way, she ignored them

6

and scratched behind my ears. I liked the way she touched and rubbed.

They made more mouth noises, then started to walk away.

"Hey, don't leave," we all yelled. "This is fun. Come on back."

They didn't listen. Despite all our wiggling and wagging and scents, they walked to look in the other pens.

But when they were just a few feet away, the woman People stopped and turned. Even with all my brothers and sisters clamoring all over one another and jumping this way and that, and even with Tiny and me on the bottom, she looked straight at me.

There was something special about that look. Something that made an excited, yet warm and easy feeling come inside. I liked her. I liked her a bunch.

After a while, they got back in their machine monster and left. The woman People looked at me one last time. I got that same warm feeling from her look, but when they left, the feeling went with them. At the time, I didn't think anymore about it.

Besides, I could always ask Mother. She would know why the woman People's look made me feel the way I did. Mother would tell me. Mother told us everything—except "leaving."

Chapter 2

I guess there are a lot of things to learn when you're little. Mother was about the best place to go to find out stuff. Of course, there were a lot of things we had known—right from the very beginning. These were things Mother didn't have to teach us because our inside feelings had already told us.

Inside, we knew stuff like—birds were the most interesting thing in the world, next to People. We'd never seen a snake, but our inside feelings told us that we didn't need to mess with them and it was best to leave the nasty things alone. Our inside feelings told us how to move our feet in deep water, although the deepest water was in the drinking bowl next to Mother's food. It only came up to our ankles.

Mother had told us to trust our feelings. Mostly she taught about People animals.

One of the most important things she had told us was that they couldn't understand Dog. No matter how much we blinked, wiggled our ears, held our tail this way and that, or gave our smells—People animals just didn't get it.

"We learn about the world with our nose," she had explained. "Our nose is the most important thing we have and we need to take good care of our nose. But when People animals learned to make mouth noises . . . well, they lost their nose. They can't talk to each other with smells. The only way they can communicate is with mouth noises."

"Do People animals howl at night like Old Blue?" I asked.

Mother frowned at me and twitched an ear. "Huh?"

"You said they lost their nose," I answered with a wiggle of my whiskers. "You told me that Old Blue lost his nose. So do people howl at night like Old Blue does?"

Mother smiled. "No. They depend on us and our nose to find quail for them."

"What are quail?" Tiny wondered.

"We are bird dogs and quail are birds," Mother answered. "But not just any bird. They have the most wonderfully delicious smell in the whole world. In fact, it's the second best smell there is."

"What's the best smell?" I asked.

"Proud."

"What's Proud?"

Mother's chest puffed really big. "It's a smell that our Mys give when they love us so much they can hardly stand it. When we find quail and point them, it makes our Mys proud. And Proud is the best smell ever!"

Mother licked us with her tongue. She fed us her delicious milk and kept us warm. Having her close always seemed to chase away the angry voices that came from the other pens or from inside the barn. Her tongue on our faces and backs covered us like a blanket and protected us from the threatening smells and frightening sounds. Curled up next to her with my brothers and sisters made me safe from all the scary things of the night.

Then, when we were two months old, Mr. Tommy had taken us away from Mother.

He and Roberto just up and snatched all six of us right out of our pen. They put us in a new place. It had dirt for a floor instead of the thick heavy wire we were used to. I liked it better because my feet didn't fall through the holes when I tried to walk around. Of course, there was always poop to step in, but if you were careful . . .

11

Anyway, I liked the dirt floor. I liked the room, too. The pen was big and we could run and chase and play until we were ready to drop.

When night came, I didn't like it. My brothers and sisters didn't either. That was because Mother wasn't there. We whined and cried and barked almost all night, but she never came. Mother loved us. We just couldn't understand why she didn't come. She'd told us that Mr. Tommy was a nice People. But if he really was nice, why would he do something so mean as making us leave Mother? It just didn't make sense. I was lonely and sad, and even with my brothers and sisters around I was a little scared, too. Worst of all, Old Blue howled at night. My mother wasn't there to chase the sad and mournful sound from my ears and from my heart.

The next day, we played and chased and wrestled. It seemed to keep our minds off of how much we missed Mother. At night, nothing helped. The next day, we played even harder— maybe tonight we'd be so tired we wouldn't have to think about Mother.

A few days went by and this big machine monster rumbled and puttered into the Big Yard. A man People got out. Mr. Tommy came and both made the People noises with their mouths. They touched their paws together and pumped their arms up and down. Then Mr. Tommy went to the barn. We had been so excited when he brought Mother out, we could hardly stand it. It was wonderful to see her again! We jumped and leaped and barked and pounced and tumbled all over each other. Chuck even fell in some poop once. But we were so happy to see Mother that nobody so much as noticed.

We got even more excited when they came to look in our pen. While Mr. Tommy and the man People made mouth noises, we told Mother how happy we were to see her and how glad we were that she was coming back to us.

"But I'm not coming back," she said with a soft smile and a twist of her tail. "You're my babies and I'll always love you. But you're growing up. I can't stay with you forever. I have to go back home with My Gary."

"Oh, please, please! Don't leave us, Mother," we all whined at once.

"Now hush that," she ordered with a squint of her eyes and a soft growl. "It's time to leave. I want to go with My Gary. I love him and he loves me. He is very proud of me. Your My People will come before too long, and you will understand."

Bobby plopped on his haunches.

"Why do you love your Gary more than us?" He whimpered. "Why are People animals so important?"

13

Mother's ears went up.

"No one knows," she answered as honestly as she could. "It has always been this way, for as long as anyone remembers. We must have People before our lives are complete.

"You are my babies." Her ears arched and she stood even taller and straighter than I had ever seen. "I am a great bird dog. Your father was a great bird dog. You will be the best bird dogs EVER. I just know it. You'll be fine."

Something about the scents she gave and the way she held herself . . . well, it made us all feel sort of big and brave. We stood straight, too. I felt my chest begin to fill . . . then suddenly, I remembered Old Blue. Inside my head, I could hear his howls from last night. The air whooshed out of my chest.

"But, Mother," I shuddered. "What if we mess up? What if something bad happens to our nose? What if we don't make our My proud? Will they stop loving us? Will they stop being our My?"

Mother didn't have time to answer. The man People tugged on her rope. She didn't pull back. She didn't even try to stay with us. With a smile and her tail waving back and forth in the air, she trotted happily behind him.

"My Gary's ready to take me home," she wagged. "I hope your life is as rich and happy as mine. Take care of your nose. Love you all. Good-bye."

We sat down and watched her hop into the tummy of a big machine monster. It roared and puttered, then it took our mother away. I wished she had time to answer my question. It was really important. It worried me—especially at night when Old Blue howled.

Chapter 3

I played with my brothers and sisters. We romped and wrestled. Beth pulled Tiny's tail and when Tiny turned to snap at her she'd run. They chased each other round and round the pen. Over the next few weeks, People came and looked at us. Ben left with a man People and his little boy. Chuck was taken by a man People, only he didn't want to go because he was afraid it really wasn't his My. Things were quiet for a few days, then more People came. Excited, we all wiggled and jumped and wagged our tails. I liked People. But none left me with the feeling that the woman People had.

Then one day, she came back.
The man People and a boy People came with

16

her. And when she looked at me, I knew what Mother had meant when she'd told us about our My.

How I knew or why . . . well . . . I just knew.

Mr. Tommy let me out of the pen. I ran straight to her and wiggled and jumped around and tried to kiss her with my tongue.

She sat on the grass with her long hind legs crossed. She held me and stroked my back.

"Come on," I wiggled and jerked. "I want to show you how fast I can run. You can run with me. It's fun. Let's go. Let's run!"

She just held me tighter and laughed with her soft voice. The man People handed Mr. Tommy some pieces of green paper, and the next thing I knew . . .

It was warm in the tummy of the big monster. The machine that swallowed us roared and shook and zoomed. It was scary. The boy People sat beside me. He was a big boy People—almost a man People, but not quite. He rubbed my back. That felt good, but not good enough to chase away the scaries or make the roar and rumble of the machine monster stop.

I could see the tops of trees every now and then. They spun past so quickly I could hardly tell they were trees. There were clouds in the sky. Like the trees, they moved too, only not as fast. It seemed like everything was whizzing and whooshing. Despite the warm feeling in the machine monster's tummy and the boy People's comforting hand on my back, I still trembled.

"We can stop now," I told them with a twitch of my ear and a jerk of my rear end.

Nobody said anything.

"You can let me out now," I suggested with one of my best smells. "I'm ready to go back and play with my brothers and sisters. Okay?"

Nothing.

Everything was whizzing and spinning. My tummy growled. I squeezed my eyes shut. Tried to think of nice things that would chase the scaries away.

It didn't work. My tummy rolled.

"I don't feel so good," I told them. "I think you should stop and let me out." I twitched and wiggled and belched. "This is serious!"

They didn't understand.

This was horrible. Terrible. I felt totally rotten. If they didn't let me out of this monster so I could get some fresh air, I was afraid . . .

I threw up.

I felt rotten! Now you've done it, I thought. Great start! How can you expect your My to love you if you throw up? Throwing up has to be the worst thing in the world—especially when you're trying to make your People like you.

My tummy rolled again.

18

Oh, no! My My is going to take me back, I thought. They're going to put me in the pen with Old Blue. Nobody will ever love me. I'm gonna end up howling at night. I'm going to . . .

I threw up again.

Suddenly, there was a whole lot of mouth noises and jumping around inside the machine monster.

"Puppy carsick, Mama?" The man People glanced back at me.

"Yeah," my My answered.

She leaned over the top of the big cloth bench at the front of the machine monster. Carefully, she pulled the towel from under me. She sort of wadded the bad stuff up inside and used a dry corner to wipe my face. Then the boy People who sat beside me picked me up gently and my My slipped a fresh towel underneath. When the boy People laid me back down, I felt a little better.

My My smiled down at me and patted my head. I closed my eyes. I didn't feel good. I cocked an ear and opened one eye. My My was still smiling and patting my head. Despite how horrible I felt, her look almost wagged my tail.

There was no doubt in my mind as I felt her look. She was my My, all right. I mean, if she could still love me after I threw up—she just had to be my My. I closed my eyes and plopped my head on the clean towel.

* * *

19

The machine monster finally shut up. When they opened the doors, the fresh air made me feel better. They got out and the boy People put me on the ground. I didn't know where I was, but I could tell I was a long long ways from home. Nothing smelled the same. Nothing looked the same. I staggered, trying to get my balance and hoping my tummy would quit rolling.

Suddenly, a strange odor caught my nose. I leaned forward sniffing at the smell.

This fuzzy gray thing appeared. He rubbed against the big black paw of the machine monster. Yellow eyes grew tight when he spotted me.

"Hi," I wagged.

He didn't wag back. I took a few steps in his direction.

All at once, the gray thing went POOF! I mean, it was like one second he was just standing there and the next second he was twice as big—like he was about to blow up or something.

It stopped me dead in my tracks. I couldn't believe my eyes.

"Hey, what happened? How did you do that?"

"Back off," the gray thing hissed. "You're a dog. I hate dogs!"

"I'm a puppy," I corrected.

"That's even worse," he sneered.

I cocked an ear and took another step. "How'd you get so big?"

The gray thing's eyes narrowed. He arched his

back and raised the paw that was closest to me. Long sharp claws sprang out.

"I mean it." His lip curled. "You come any closer, I'm gonna rip your nose off."

I leaned closer. "You're not a dog, are you? If you'll just let me get close enough for one good smell . . ."

Before I could even blink, his paw flashed out. Then the other paw—both whacked me on the tip of the nose. I jumped so hard that I tumbled backward over my own tail. I ended up on my back with my feet in the air. I had to struggle to get to my feet, and just about the time I stood up, the pain hit.

It was like my nose was on fire.

"Oooouch!" I squealed. "That hurt! You really did . . . you ripped my nose off."

The boy People swooped me up in his arms and kicked at the gray thing. He didn't really hit him with his foot, but it scared him away. He tucked his tail, raced around the side of the machine monster, and climbed a big tree beside the People house.

Whimpering and crying, I crossed my eyes and looked down at the tip of my nose. It really wasn't gone. But there were two deep scratch marks right on the tip of my snout. It hurt! A little blood began to leak from the marks. It made me cry.

The boy People patted my head and the man

21

People and my My talked to me real sweet. They carried me away from the machine monster and the tree where the gray thing glared down and swished his tail at me.

I heard a squeaking sound when they opened a gate. The boy People put me on the ground inside a small yard. There was a chain-link fence on one side, a lot like the fence at our kennel. On two other sides were black poles that went up and down to make another fence, and on the fourth side of the little yard was the People house made of brick. The boy People and my My went inside. The man People put a little white stick in his mouth. He coughed when he stuck fire to the end of it and blew smoke out of his face. Then he sat down in a chair and blew more smoke.

With one eye on the tree where the gray thing went, I'd just started to explore the little yard when I heard the door open.

I glanced around and saw a dog. I'd never been so happy to see another dog in my whole life. He was about the same size as me, only kind of fat. Fact was, he was so big around he waddled when he walked toward me. He had short white hair on his back, and fuzzy, kind of long hair on his chest and tummy. It hung down like a skirt that women People sometimes wear. His ears were sharp and pointy and long hair drooped from his chin and jaws, kind of like Mr. Tommy's beard.

"Hi," I wagged. "Did you see what just hap-

23

pened? This big, gray, fuzzy thing—he tried to rip my nose off. You should have been here. I mean, no reason at all, he just up and swatted me and . . ."

"What are you doing in MY yard?" he growled.

"Huh . . . who, me?" I stammered. "I . . . er . . ."

"This is MY yard. GET OUT!"

I wagged my tail and took another step toward him. "No, wait. You don't understand. This big gray thing . . . out there . . . and he . . ."

"You don't get out, I'll bite your head off."

"But . . . but . . ."

Short, stubby legs popped like springs. The dog took one little hop. I saw the white as his teeth flashed. Before I could jerk back . . .

HE BIT ME—right on the very tip of my nose!

Chapter 4

Being the "new kid" was NOT cool.

The gray thing scratched my nose. The dog bit my nose. Even though the People yelled at him and the boy People swatted him on the bottom and chased him back in the house, my nose still hurt. The People didn't like me, either—I guess. They just played with me for a little while before they went back inside.

I crossed my eyes and looked down my snout. My poor nose was starting to swell. It throbbed and pounded like somebody was whacking it with a stick. I was all alone with nothing to do.

Despite my sore nose, I sniffed at the black fence around the little yard. There was plenty of room between the up and down poles, so I squeezed through and went to explore.

Another fence surrounded a big yard. The fence was made of chain link, just like our pens back home. Only this pen was ENORMOUS. None of the cages back at the kennel were nearly this big. The little yard was almost all concrete. Here, there was grass everywhere. I liked grass. There were trees, too. I followed the fence to the big trees at the left corner of the yard. Not far from the trees was a wood thing with plants growing in it. I trotted over and sniffed at the pink flowers that stood at the top of the plants. They smelled sweet, but I was careful not to get my nose too close when I saw the thorns. My nose hurt bad enough as it was. If one of those thorns stuck me . . .

There was another tree at the right corner of the yard. But instead of having a brown trunk, this one was green from the very bottom clear to the very top. It didn't have leaves. It had sharp, pointed green needles all over it. I started over to investigate.

Suddenly, I froze in my tracks. My ears perked so high, the loose floppy skin around my neck almost choked me. My eyes got as big around as Mother's food bowl.

Right in the middle of all that grass in the big yard was concrete. And right in the middle of all that concrete was the most HUMONGOUS drinking bowl I had ever seen.

I inched closer—one step at a time.

My toenails scraped the concrete. Still keeping my hind feet on the grass, I leaned forward and sniffed. The water smelled funny. Not clean, fresh water that was good for drinking, this stuff made my nose sting and twitch. It was deep, too. The water was really clear and I could see all the way to the bottom. A little bark slipped from my throat when I realized that there was enough water in this drinking bowl to swallow me, my brothers and sisters, and all the dogs at Mr. Tommy's kennel. I plopped on my haunches and looked at it.

Why would anybody need such an enormous drinking bowl? I wondered.

"BUZZZZZ!"

The sudden sound startled me. I sprang to my feet and spun around. A bug landed on one of the sweet-smelling pink flowers that stood in a row along the back fence. "Buzzz," he said with his fluttering wings.

I cocked an ear and tilted my head. The bug stuck his head down inside of one of the pink flowers.

"What you doing?" I asked.

"Buzzz."

"I'm a puppy. I just got here. But I want to go home 'cause nobody likes me."

He didn't answer. Instead, he just stuck his head deeper into the pink flower. I moved a step or two toward him. "This fuzzy gray thing

27

scratched my nose, then the dog bit me. My nose really hurts."

"Buzzz." He fluttered his wings and moved to another flower. The bug was sort of a bright red color with black wings. I couldn't see his face because he had it stuck down into one of the flowers, but his back end was kind of long and pointy.

I moved closer.

"Do you want to be my friend?"

"Buzzz."

"I could really use a friend right now." I confessed with a sigh. My head tilted in the other direction as I took another step toward him. "What'ya doin' in that flower?"

"Buzzz." He ignored me and flew a little ways to another pink flower.

I remember Mother telling us that we couldn't understand bugs. Still, I was really lonely, and the way this guy was moving from flower to flower and working so hard, it really made me curious.

"Are you getting something to eat? Are you playing down in there?"

"Buzzz."

Both ears shrugged. I couldn't understand buzzz, but maybe if I got close enough to smell— to look down in that pink flower and see what he was doing with his head down in there . . .

I stepped up right beside the bush with the

pink flowers. I leaned forward, easy and careful so I wouldn't startle him. I got closer and closer and closer until my nose was almost touching his rump.

Suddenly, his head popped from the flower. Big, bubblelike eyes glared at me.

"BUZZZ!" His back end whipped around. This sharp, pointy thing stuck out like a tail and . . .

WHAM!

He jabbed the pointy thing right into the tip of my nose.

"Yipe, yipe, yipe!" I screamed and jumped back.

I blinked. I felt water leak out of my eyes and trickle down my cheeks. I shook my head.

When the gray thing scratched me, it hurt. When the dog bit me, that really hurt. But this . . .

"Yipe, yipe, yipe," I cried again.

It just kept right on hurting. My nose got hotter and hotter and I couldn't stand it. I shook my head until my ears flopped. I backed up, but it didn't help. Frantically, I rubbed my nose with my paw. It didn't help, either. It just hurt more and more.

"Yipe!" I screamed. I had to get away from the hurt. I couldn't stand it. I wheeled around and ran away, fast as I could go.

Only, I didn't go very far. Suddenly, there was

29

no ground under my feet. I was falling . . . falling . . .

All at once, I was in water. I couldn't breathe. Instantly, my inside feelings took over. My feet paddled and churned, all four working like mad.

My head popped above the surface and I gulped down a deep breath. Frantically, I kept pawing the water. No matter how much I paddled and pawed, I couldn't touch the bottom. I swam back to the side where I'd fallen in, but concrete was too far away. I couldn't reach it. I couldn't get out.

My legs dug the water harder. I turned and paddled to the other side. There was still nothing to grab hold of—still no way out.

I paddled and paddled. My legs were getting tired. I could hardly breathe. Legs churning and sides pumping in and out as I gasped for air, I headed for the other end of the enormous drinking bowl.

It was a long way off, and by the time I got there I was exhausted. My legs felt like they were going to drop off. My head and ears were sinking lower and lower. My nose was barely above the surface.

This was it. This was the end. I was such a happy puppy. I liked my brothers and sisters. I loved my mother. I finally had my My—but now it was all over. I was a goner. And what a way to go—to drown in a drinking bowl . . .

31

Chapter 5

*A*big paw caught me under my chest and belly. The paw lifted me.

I kept paddling.

Even when I was clear out of the water and pawing nothing but air, I kept paddling.

The man People looked at me and shook his head. "Dumb mutt," he sighed. "You're a pointer, not a retriever. You're not supposed to get in the swimming pool."

Dangling in midair, I kept right on paddling until the man People wrapped both paws around me and held me against his chest. My legs were so tired and weak, I could barely move them. Still desperate to get away from all that water, I climbed up his chest and was going clear to the top of his head. I wanted to get as far away from that drinking bowl as I could. But when my front paws draped over his shoulders, he hugged me tight and I couldn't move. I was as high as I was gonna go.

I peeked over his shoulder and looked down. The water in the drinking bowl sloshed and splashed below us as he turned and carried me toward the People house.

"What happened?" I heard my My's voice, but I was so tired I couldn't even turn around and look at her.

"Puppy was sniffin' at a wasp that landed on one of the rosebushes." When the man People talked, I could feel his chest rumble against mine. "Thing stung him on the nose and he ran. Fell smack into the swimming pool. Get some towels."

The man People, the boy People and my My took turns holding me on their laps and rubbing me with these big pieces of cloth. I wasn't really cold, but I couldn't stop shivering. They rubbed and rubbed and rubbed until I was finally dry. I quit shaking.

Then they went inside the People house.

It wasn't long before dark shadows began to stretch across the big yard. I didn't even think about squeezing through the black fence. I sat as close to the People house as I could get. It got darker and darker. I pressed harder against the brick.

Suddenly, light flooded the concrete place where I lay. It went out in kind of a half ring into the big dark yard. I raised my head and looked around. There was a clicking sound behind me. I turned my head and cocked an ear. The door swung open. Cool air rushed out bringing strange smells from inside. People noises came to my ears and perked them up as my My stepped over me.

She reached down and patted my head when I sniffed her leg. "Hello, J.C." Her voice made me feel a little better. My tail wagged just a bit.

I followed her to the edge of the hard gray concrete. She put a bowl down. It smelled good. It was food. Water came to my mouth and my tail whipped back and forth. It was food like back home. Real honest-to-goodness food like my brothers and sisters and I ate. When I bit into it, I found that there was more. There was some sort of red chewy stuff in there with the food. That was REALLY good.

I gobbled it down while my My patted me and watched. She kept talking to me and saying "J.C." over and over again.

The man People came out and sat in one of the People chairs. He scratched a piece of wood on a tiny box and a fire puffed up. He stuck it to a white stick that hung from his mouth, then blew the fire away. Smoke came from the white stick. It smelled nasty.

He puffed on the nasty stick until I was finished with my supper. When he ground the glowing red end of it into a bowl, I went to check it out. There was gray powdery stuff in there and the ends of a whole bunch of those nasty sticks. I could barely use my nose because it had started to swell. I sniffed but only a little air got in. The stuff in the bowl smelled even worse than the smoke. It hurt my nose, then tickled. I sneezed.

The man People petted me and I forgot all about the stinky bowl full of nasty sticks. Beyond the half circle of light where we sat, it was really dark now.

"I'm sure glad you're out here with me." My tail thumped the concrete. "I don't like being alone, especially in the dark. For a while there I thought I was gonna have to sleep by myself. I've never slept by myself before. I don't think I'd like that too much."

The man People made a grunting sound and got up from the chair.

"Hey, wait. Where you going?"

He reached for the door.

I darted in front of him so he couldn't open it. "Hold on just a minute. You're not gonna go inside and leave me, are you? I mean, like, it's really dark out here and there's all sorts of strange sounds and smells and noises and . . ."

He shoved me aside with his leg and closed the door—right smack-dab in my face.

I stood on my hind legs and put my paws on the door. Maybe if he saw me he'd open up and come back out. "Please don't leave me out here all alone. I'm scared. My nose hurts. I've always had someone to sleep beside me. I don't want to sleep all by myself. Oh, please, please, please . . ."

Much to my relief, it wasn't long before the door opened and the People came outside again. They brought the dog with them.

Careful to keep my nose out of reach, I eased over to him. "Hi," I greeted timidly with my happiest smell and wag.

"Chomps, be nice," the man People warned from behind the closed door.

The dog just stuck his nose in the air and ignored me.

The man People blew smoke from one of his nasty sticks. The boy People and my My sat in chairs next to him and made People noises. The dog trotted to the fence and raised his leg. When he was done, he kicked grass at the wet spot with his hind feet.

I walked slowly toward him.

"I'm sorry I'm in your yard," I told him with my eyes and a twitch of my whiskers. "It's not my fault. The People brought me here. Please don't be mad at me. Please don't bite me again."

He sniffed at me. A ridge of hair rose down his back. "Beat it, kid," he growled.

"Chomps!" The man People roared.

Quickly, the dog tucked his tail and backed away. My My opened the door and let Chomps Dog back in the house. As soon as he was gone, I trotted over to the man People.

"You're really nice," I wagged. "You saved me from the big drinking bowl. You told the Chomps Dog not to bite me. Thank you."

I stood on my hind legs and put my front paws in his lap. "Thank you, thank you, thank you!"

He smiled down and patted my head. His touch felt good. I felt safe from the drinking bowl and from Chomps Dog and from the dark that lurked just outside our half circle of light.

"If you'll stay out here with me, I'll be really good. I won't bark or growl or make bad smells. I don't want to be alone. Please?"

He patted me again. I wanted to be closer to him. I pulled with my front paws and kicked with my hind feet. If I could just get up there . . . if I could just get to his lap . . . I pulled harder. I climbed with all my might.

Then his big paw slipped under my rump and he lifted me. The night was scary. My new home was scary. And even though I felt safe in the man People's lap, I still trembled.

"J.C. Puppy's had a pretty rough day." The man People's voice rumbled.

"Sure has," my My agreed. "I never dreamed he could squeeze through the security fence, much less that he'd fall in the pool. If you hadn't come out for a cigarette when you did, the little thing might have drowned."

I felt safe on the man People's lap. Still, a shudder raced through me.

"Think he's a little scared, too," the man People said. "I bet J.C.'s never been alone much. He's always had his brothers and sisters to sleep with."

My My nodded her head. "Sure hate for him to end up in the pool again. And with no one out here to watch him . . ."

The boy People leaned toward her. "Why don't we let him sleep in the house tonight?" he suggested.

The man People and my My both looked at him and smiled. "Bet he'd feel safe and happy if he had somebody to sleep with," my My almost laughed.

Suddenly, the boy People's eyes got really big. "Now, wait. Hold on," he said, waving both arms at them. "I meant in the playroom or the kitchen or . . ."

The man People and my My looked at him and smiled, even bigger than before. The air kind of whooshed out of the boy People's chest.

"Ah, man . . . I can't believe it."

Chapter 6

I couldn't believe it, either. This was GREAT!

Never before had I seen the inside of a People house, much less been in one. But that's just what happened. And even better—I didn't have to sleep all by myself.

The boy was named Justin. I slept with him. We didn't sleep on the cold, hard ground, though. Instead, he tossed me onto this big mat that was far above the floor. At first, I didn't like it. The thing made a sloshing sound when I landed on it. When Justin bounced or flopped around on the mat, it went up and down and made the same sloshing noise that kind of reminded me of the big drinking bowl where I had almost drowned.

For a time, he let me walk around and explore on the big mat. It really felt weird when I walked.

I eased to the edge and looked down at the floor. It was a long ways, so I decided not to jump. He wrestled with me and played with me for a while. That was fun. He laughed when I licked him in the face. He yelled and shoved me around if I bit his big paws or chewed on his arm.

After a while, he got quiet. Then there was a click sound and the light went out. I wanted to play some more. He shoved me down beside him. I tried to crawl up and lick his face. He shoved me down. I tried to go explore. He shoved me down. This time, he held me. One of his big arms wrapped around me from underneath and his paw held my shoulders. His other arm draped over my back and held my bottom. Every time I tried to move, he just hugged me tighter.

The People house was a whole new world. There were a million things to do and places to sniff and explore. But soon, when I finally figured out I couldn't move or go anyplace, I settled down.

It had been a long day. I didn't realize how tired I was until I lay still for a moment or two. My eyes felt heavy. Before I knew it, I was asleep.

The man People came for me early the next morning. My Justin was still asleep and I had just squeezed from under his big paw that was draped across my back. I hadn't even gotten to the edge of the bed when the man People swooped me up in his arms and carried me outside. He put me on the ground, patted my back and said, "Tee-tee, Puppy."

I tried to sniff the grass. That's when I saw my nose. When I looked down my snout, I almost fell over. My poor nose was nearly twice as big as it was supposed to be. It hurt, too. Well, not bad. It only hurt when I tried to take a deep breath or sniff something.

"Tee-tee, Puppy," the man People said again.

He kept saying it over and over. For a while, I thought they must have changed my name while I was asleep. But after I walked around a moment or two and went to the bathroom, he picked me up and patted me.

"Good boy, J.C.! Good puppy! J.C.'s a good, good boy!"

I could tell he was happy. Why, I didn't know, but I liked the way he petted me and the way his mouth noises made me feel.

He plopped his rump in the chair and let me sit in his lap. I liked that, too.

What I didn't like was when he stuck one of those nasty sticks in his face and blew smoke. My nose was so big, I could hardly smell anything with it. I *could* smell that nasty smoke, though. My nose hurt as it was, and the sharp smell from the man People's nasty sticks didn't help.

I got down from his lap and went to explore.

41

It was a little hard to do. I could always learn more about things and places with my nose. But since my nose hardly worked, I had to use my eyes and ears.

From the trees near the silver barn, I could hear birds chirping. My eyes could see them fluttering and jumping from branch to branch, if I watched really close. I heard the man People go inside the house and shut the door. I saw a grayish brown bird with a long tail and white on its wings land in the tree with the green needles. Then another bird flew into the tree. She had a bug in her mouth.

Suddenly, there was a whole bunch of chirping.

"Me, me!" the chirping said. "That's my bug. You had the last one. Feed me. Me!"

Then the chirping stopped and the birds flew away. In just a moment they were back with more bugs. Then, from a dark spot from inside the tree, the chirping started again.

"Oh boy, two bugs. Mine. Mine. Feed me. Feed me!"

I eased to the edge of the black poles that surrounded the concrete. My head would fit through just fine. So would the rest of me. Still, I remembered the bug with the sharp tail and the big drinking bowl. I hesitated, but for only a second. The birds and all their chirping were just too exciting. I simply had to go see what was going on.

So I slipped between the black bars. I saw the

big drinking bowl. I made a picture of it in my mind so I would be sure not to get too close to it—no matter what happened. Then I concentrated on the tree.

The big birds came back with more bugs. There was more chirping and yelling from inside the tree. When they swooped away I eased closer.

High up in the tree was a bundle of twigs and grass. It was shaped a little like the food bowl my My fed me in last night, only much, much smaller. The chirping came from inside.

Why I didn't rush up to the tree and put my paws on a branch so I could see better, I don't know. There was something inside me—one of those inside feelings that told me to be very quiet. One step at a time, careful not to make a sound, I sneaked up to the tree. Only inches from the base, I stopped.

I heard a fluttering sound. Then a boastful chirp.

"I'm ready. This time I'm gonna do it," the chirp said.

"Well, go," another chirp answered.

"I will. Just give me a second."

"Quit talking about it and do it."

"I will. Just give me time. I'm almost . . . hey, quit. Stop pushin'. Don't . . . Oh, NO! AHHhhh . . ."

All of a sudden, there was a clunking sound from up in the tree. There was fluttering and

43

more clunking and a loud thud. A bird landed right in front of me. Well, he didn't land. He sort of flopped flat on his back. I cocked my head to the side and stared down at him.

I'd never been this close to a bird before. I'd seen them plenty of times, up in the trees or flying to the top of the barn back home. But never, never this close. I tilted my head the other direction and leaned to sniff him. The bird rolled over and got to his feet. He fluttered his wings and kind of shook himself.

"Man, what a trip." He bobbed his head up and down and shook once more. "Hey, Charlie," he called to the tree. "Watch that first step. It's a doozie."

My nose almost touched him. Still, it was so swollen and puffy I couldn't smell anything. I sucked in a deep breath, trying to get a sniff.

Suddenly, his eyes flashed.

"EEeeeee . . ." He screamed. "A monster!"

I snapped my head to the side so I could see it. When I didn't see the monster, I turned the other direction.

"What monster?" I gasped. "Where?"

"Help! Help! The monster's gonna eat me!"

I looked all around, but there just wasn't any monster. So I leaned back toward the little bird and tried to get a better smell.

"You're nuts," I told him. "There's no monster. You and me are the only ones out here."

There was a swishing sound, and out of the corner of my right eye I saw a grayish brown streak. Wings opened and I got a glimpse of white feathers. Before I could even tilt my head to look up at it . . .

WHAM!

Mama bird bit me. Right smack-dab on the tip of my sore nose.

The pain was horrible. It knocked me backward. Head over paws, I tumbled. My tail crunched under me, then my head went *thunk* on the hard ground. It took me a moment to get on my feet. I crossed my eyes and looked down my snout. My nose throbbed and pounded. Water leaked from my eyes.

"You big, bad monster," the mama bird scolded. "You leave my baby alone!"

"I'm not a monster. I'm a bird dog."

She held her wings out so she'd look big and mean. "Go on and get out of here. Leave my baby alone or I'll peck you again."

Crying from the pain, I tucked my tail and ran for the safety of the People house and the man People's lap.

Chapter 7

I learned a whole bunch in the next few weeks. First off, I learned that when your nose gets scratched by a cat *and* bit by a dog, *and* stung by a wasp, ***and*** pecked by a bird that it swells up really, REALLY big!

For a while, my nose was so huge that I could barely see around it. I couldn't run and play much because I couldn't see where I was going. I was afraid I might run into something. That would make it hurt even more. Mostly I was afraid that I would lose my nose like Old Blue lost his. I made myself a promise that if my nose was okay, I would always take good care of it. I would never, *never* let anything hurt my nose again.

It took a week for the swelling to go down and two weeks before my nose started to work again.

I also learned that my My was named Carol. My Carol fed me and petted me and talked sweet to me. The boy People, called Justin, was my My, too. That's because he loved me. My Justin was full of play and fun. He chased me around the big yard and wrestled with me and laughed when I chased him. I learned that when it was time for bed, if I curled up next to My Justin and lay really still, he wouldn't push me down or clunk me over the head with his pillow.

The man People was named Bill. He was my My as well. He saved me from the enormous drinking bowl, and he talked my Justin into letting me sleep inside at night. When I was scared or hurt, all I had to do was go put my paws on My Bill's leg and he'd lift me up onto his lap and pet me and love me. I didn't like the smoke that came from his nasty sticks, but just being close to him and sitting on his lap was almost enough to make me forget about the stink.

Another thing I figured out was that Gray Cat and Chomps weren't as mean and tough as I first thought.

Gray Cat was a hunter. He caught birds, mice, and rats—mostly rats. He would catch them out by the silver barn. Then he would eat part of them and leave other parts just outside the door to the People house. That was to show My Carol what a great hunter he was. When she woke up in the mornings, she would take me outside.

Sometimes she would look to see if Gray Cat had brought her a present. Other times, she would forget and almost step on the rat parts. Then she would tell Gray Cat what a good mouser he was and pet him. After he went inside, her nose would kind of crinkle up and she'd use a long stick to throw the rat parts way out past the fence. Gray Cat did most of his hunting at night, and during the day all he wanted to do was sleep. I learned that if I didn't startle him or get too close, he wouldn't swat at me with his paw, and he was really pretty nice.

Chomps was a soccer dog. Well, he was really a Scottie, but he was a soccer Scottie. (I guess soccer's big in Scotland.) Anyway, My Justin would come outside every morning with this round black-and-white ball. He'd kick it and chase it around the yard or bounce it up and down on his paw or head or knee. After a while, he would open the black gate with the up-and-down bars and let Chomps come out with him.

My Justin and Chomps played keep-away with the soccer ball. My Justin would kick it with his paw and run round and round the enormous drinking bowl. Chomps would growl at the ball and bite it or try to trap it between his front paws. If he got it, My Justin would put his paw on top of the ball, spin around, and start kicking it in the other direction to keep Chomps from getting it. They laughed and played and ran and ran and ran.

When they were through, they came back in the little yard with the black poles and sat down. They were both panting and out of breath, but Chomps picked up his Wiggie and wanted My Justin to play some more.

Wiggie was a short, fat piece of rope with two knots on either end. Chomps got it in his mouth, growled, and shook it. Then he took it to My Justin and put his paws in My Justin's lap. My Justin ignored him.

"Ah, come on and play," Chomps wagged.

My Justin still ignored him.

"I'll play with you," I said as I trotted up beside them.

"Beat it!" Chomps growled.

I tucked my tail, but before I could back away, My Justin got one end of the rope and began to tug.

"I got it," Chomps growled. "You can't get it away from me. I'm gonna hang onto it forever." Only this growl was different from the growl he used on me. This was a play-growl—teasing and fun.

My Justin pulled and played with him and Wiggie. Then he put one end of Wiggie against the corner of my mouth.

Cautiously, I took it and bit down on the knot.

"Man, you're no match for me," Chomps said

in his play-growl. "I'll drag your tail all over this yard. I'll . . ."

He began to tug and yank. I hung on.

Sure enough, he dragged me all over the yard. We were both about the same size, but Chomps was much older and stronger. Still, it was fun. If I lost my end of Wiggie, Chomps would take off around the yard and I had to chase him. After a while, My Justin opened the gate and let us run and play in the big yard. I was careful not to get too close to the enormous drinking bowl when Chomps and I played tug-of-war with the Wiggie or when I chased him round and round.

I could tell when Chomps was tired of the Wiggie game. The tone of his growl changed. Whenever I heard that, I'd let go of the Wiggie—real quick—to keep from getting my nose bit again.

I learned that as long as I listened and minded him, Chomps was fun to play with. Mostly, he liked to sleep in the sun. But almost every day we played and tugged on the Wiggie and chased and ran. Inside, we played and wrestled on the People bed or on the floor. My Carol and My Justin and My Bill would laugh at us. Sometimes, they even played with us.

I learned that it made my Mys happy if I went to the bathroom, *outside*, when they said "tee-tee Puppy." They were *not* happy if I forgot and

51

made a mess inside the People house. It also made my Mys happy if I came to them when they whistled and said, "Here, J.C. Puppy." I learned that the enormous drinking bowl was really a swimming pool. My Mys would jump in and splash and paddle from one end to the other. Once, they made me get in it, too. They put me on a pad that floated. My feet got wet and I shook and trembled. But they talked sweet to me and didn't shove me off the pad and into the water. I didn't like the pool much. I think they could tell because they finally let me off the pad. It felt good to have my feet on solid ground.

I learned that potato chips were good. They tasted even better than my puppy food. I learned that the vet was bad. The vet was a big gray building made of blocks. When I went there this lady named Miss Becky pushed and poked me. She looked in my ears and took my temperature. (That was embarrassing.) Then she stabbed me with this sharp, pointed needle that really hurt, and patted me on the head. Going to the vet wasn't fun. When I got home, I learned that snapping at flies *was fun* and that they wouldn't hurt my nose.

Like I said, I learned a whole bunch of stuff. The bestest thing I learned was "go for a walk."

One evening while My Justin was watching TV, I went to lie on the People bed with My Carol. Sometimes, My Justin wasn't ready to go to bed when I was and it was fun to spend time with her. She munched on some potato chips and gave me some. Suddenly, she crunched the sack shut and jumped out of bed.

She stood in front of this bright shiny piece of glass and patted her tummy. Then she used her muscles to pull her tummy in, only when she relaxed, it sort of popped out and she patted it again. She frowned, made a growling sound at the shiny glass, then got foot covers for her paws out of the closet.

The next morning, when I was doing my tee-tee Puppy bit, she frowned down at Chomps. She patted his tummy, then patted her own.

"That's it, Chomps." She made a people noise. "I've had enough of this fat stuff. We're gonna start walking. Ready to go for a walk?"

"Go for a walk" was the best mouth noise People can make. Because "go for a walk" is the funnest thing in the whole entire world.

Chapter 8

I never got to explore outside the big yard where the enormous drinking bowl—I mean pool—was. But "go for a walk" meant that early each morning, My Carol would open the gate and I could go anyplace we wanted.

Well, almost anyplace.

There was a road behind our People house. It was covered with tiny rocks and there was tall grass on either side of it. We walked up a hill, across a long flat place, around a curve, and stopped at a big silver-colored drinking bowl.

"Is that for a big dog?" I asked Chomps.

"Man, puppies sure are dumb." He snorted at me. "That's a drinking bowl for the cows."

"Cows? What are cows?"

"They're these big animals who live behind the People house."

"Do they eat puppies?" I asked, cocking an ear. "Are they mean?"

"They eat grass." He went to sniff at something on the ground. "And they're not mean unless you get too close to their babies. You get too close and they try to stomp on you or butt you with their heads. You leave 'em alone, they're okay."

At the cow drinking bowl, we turned around and walked back to the People house. Then we went back to the drinking bowl. Five times we went back and forth and back and forth.

Each time we walked, I noticed new smells. There were animals who lived in the tall grass. Animals with strange scents that tweaked my nose and made me want to go closer to find out more about them.

Only trouble was, I was too little. If I left the road, the grass was so tall and thick I couldn't get through it or jump over it. Sticks and twigs caught my paws and tripped me. I fell flat on my snout every time I tried to go into that marvelous place to explore.

But by the end of summer, a lot of changes had taken place. First off, we didn't "go for a walk" in the mornings. That was because My Carol and My Justin had to get dressed and go to this place called school. They were gone most of the day and it wasn't much fun not having them around to play with.

My Bill didn't go to the place called school. He went in a little room and punched at keys on a machine. Sometimes, he would let me inside with him. He wouldn't let me climb up in his lap, but I could lie on the floor. As he punched his keys, I could sense his feelings. Sometimes he was happy, sometimes I could feel excitement and adventure. Other times he was sad. All this from doing nothing more than sitting behind his little machine and punching the keys. It was weird.

When My Carol came home after school . . . well, that's when the adventure really started.

Now that summer was almost over, I was bigger and stronger and braver. I didn't have to stay on the road with My Carol and My Bill when we walked. I could leap through the tall grass and go all over the farm where we lived. There were all sorts of smells—cows and skunks, birds and rabbits, places where coyotes had been during the night—the smells were wonderful and exciting. Especially the bird smells. Sometimes, I could hear a rat or mouse scurrying through the grass. When I did, I'd freeze and listen. If I heard him again, I'd go dig around where the sound came from, trying to catch him.

Now and then I'd find something dead. Dead

things smell great. They're like perfume! I'd roll in the dead thing and rub my sides on it so I could get the good smell all over me.

For some strange reason, every time I found dead things to roll in, I got a bath when we went home. I didn't much like baths. My Carol would put me in this big slippery thing with water in it. I didn't like getting wet all over. Then she'd put this stuff on me that bubbled and smelled horrible. Once I got it in my eyes. That hurt something terrible. She'd rub and rub and then wash all the bubbly stuff off.

When she let me out of the water, she and My Justin or My Bill rubbed me all over with towels. Then they sniffed me and made happy mouth noises. I don't know why they were so happy. When they washed the dead-stuff perfume off, I didn't smell very good.

I guess it was worth it to get to sleep on the waterbed, though. I liked my waterbed. I liked being inside the People house. I loved exploring in the tall grass. I was one lucky dog.

Then, one day . . .

My Carol came home from school. My Justin had to go to this thing called soccer practice, so he didn't get home until later. He was always tired and smelled sweaty so he didn't want to "go for a walk" when he came in.

My Carol put her school things away and she and My Bill got dressed to "go for a walk." It took them forever.

I ran to the door, back to the bed, then back to the door again. Finally, they opened the door. Chomps and I shot out and put our paws on the back gate. They opened the gate for us.

Hard as I could, I raced for the tall grass. I was so excited to be out and free, I could hardly stand it. I leaped into the grass and began to sniff. The coyotes had come during the night. Their scent was everywhere. Gray Cat almost caught a rabbit. It was before the coyotes had come, but it was a close call for the rabbit. The scent of fear was still strong.

It was so good to be free. So wonderful to run and chase and smell and explore. This was heaven!

Then it happened.

I needed to check and see where My Carol was. The bottom wire at the place where I came to the fence was so low, I decided to step over it instead of trying to crawl under and scratch my back. I ducked to miss the second wire.

Suddenly, something bit my ear. It was sharp. It hurt. I was running so fast, I couldn't stop. The flesh on the top of my ear ripped. Then whatever bit me pulled me to a dead stop so quickly that my feet flipped clear out from under me. I landed on my side and heard the fence wire go *twang*.

The pain made me yell. I struggled to my feet. Shaking my head, I tried to make the hurt go away. It wouldn't, so I raced for My Carol. She would help the hurt go away. My Carol loved me.

Chapter 9

"**M**ust have caught it on the barbed wire," My Bill said, holding me down.

"Looks horrible." My Carol shuddered and got to her feet. She turned her head. "Does it need stitches?"

"I don't know," he answered. "What do you think?"

"I can't look at it." Her voice sounded sad and scared.

I wiggled, trying to get free. My Bill wouldn't let me go. I shoved with my legs, trying to get up. "It doesn't hurt anymore," I tried to tell him. "It's okay, honest. Besides, I can smell a bird. Come on. Let me up."

He latched on to my ear again and held it out

from my head. It hurt, but I figured if I yelled he'd never let me go.

"I can't tell," he sighed.

My Carol started walking toward the People house. "We better take him to the vet."

My Bill finally let me loose and I took off for the smell that kept tugging at my nose. But before I knew it, I heard the gate open.

My head tilted and my good ear cocked.

They're at the house? What's going on? We just got started. My tail was perfectly still. Both ears were up—away from my head so I could hear. The chain-link gate rattled. My Bill whistled. "J.C. Here, boy!"

What were they doing at the house? I wondered. I better go check this out.

When I got home, Chomps was in the backyard. He trotted around the pool, holding the Wiggie and waiting for someone to play chase with him. When I got to the gate, My Bill opened it for me.

I smiled up and wagged my tail. "What's going on? Why did we come to the house? Chomps in trouble or somethin'? What's the deal?"

As usual, he didn't understand. He just closed the gate behind me, and without a word went into the house.

"What's going on?" I asked Chomps.

"Got me," he shrugged his ears. "Maybe it's time for supper."

"You're always thinking about eating," I let my tail droop. "It's too early for supper."

The door opened and My Carol came out. My tail jerked up again and started to wag because I figured we were going to finish our walk.

Only, before I knew it, she knelt and put a leather strap around my neck. That stopped my tail dead in midswing. I hated the leather strap. When they put that on, the rope always came next. Somebody was always yanking on the darned thing. If I tried to run or go sniff something, I couldn't. It choked me and made me cough.

Next thing I knew, we were in the old bouncy machine monster. My Carol held me next to her with an arm around me. The noisy thing roared and sputtered before we took off. Since the day I came to live with my Mys, I'd almost gotten used to the machine monsters. We'd gone for a number of rides. Sometimes I liked the machine monster. Sometimes I didn't.

Trouble with the machine monster was, I never knew where it was taking us. The last few times I had gotten to go for a ride, we went to a new place. I got to get out and run and sniff and explore while My Bill and My Justin yelled at me and followed me around. That was fun.

But in the back of my mind, I could remember another time when they took me for a ride. That time we went to this big building made of gray blocks. My People called it "the vet."

The vet smelled funny. There were cats and dogs there. I couldn't see them, but I could smell from under the door in the little room. Some were mad and some were scared and some were very, very sick. There were other smells in that room—strange, sharp smells that hurt my nose and made me want to lick myself to get the nasty taste out of my mouth.

Man, I sure hoped we weren't going there.

We stopped at the building with the gray blocks.

I didn't want to go inside. My Carol dragged me. I jerked and jumped, but the leather strap choked me, so I went.

It wasn't as bad as I remembered. This time, Miss Becky just looked at my ear. She didn't take my temperature. I was glad. She only gave My Carol some cream stuff and we got back in the truck.

My Carol put the cream on my ear. It hurt a little when she touched it, but when she was finished it didn't sting or anything. This was great. Now, maybe we could finish our walk.

We didn't walk. Instead, My Justin drove up in his machine monster just about the time we got home. I was the first to get out. I was ready to run and play. I loved My Justin and could hardly wait to get my paws on him.

I hit the end of the rope so hard that I thought the leather strap was going to hang me. No matter how much I wagged my tail and jerked and jumped, My Carol wouldn't let me go. She held on to the rope and we all followed My Justin into the house.

My Bill and My Carol told him about my ear. He looked at it and shook his head. Then he patted me.

"You call Tommy today?" he asked My Bill.

"Yeah," he answered. "Tommy said any time we were ready to bring him it'd be fine."

My Justin folded his arms. "But is he ready?"

"Tommy thinks so," My Bill shrugged. "He's your dog. Yours and Carol's. You two have to decide."

My Justin looked at me a long long time. Finally, he took a deep breath. "Let's do it."

"When," My Bill asked.

"Right now. I don't want to think about it. Let's just take him, now."

My Justin got some sunflower seeds from a package and plopped them in his mouth. My Carol went to the cold box and looked inside for a long time, only she didn't get anything out. My Bill grabbed a nasty stick and went outside.

Nobody was paying any attention to me or petting me, so I went to the bedroom and got the

Wiggie. When I came back, they were all talking again. My Justin lay down on the floor and patted me and loved on me.

It made my tail go thump on the carpet and I couldn't keep my feet still. It felt so good, I forgot all about Wiggie. I licked him and kissed him.

Only instead of laughing and pushing me away, like he usually did, he only loved me more and hugged me tighter. My Bill jingled something in his hand.

"Ready. You two sure about this?"

My Carol and My Justin didn't answer.

A strange smell—a feeling—came to my nose when My Carol knelt down on the floor beside us. She rubbed my head and stroked my back. The smell, the feeling, was scary. Still, I could feel her love inside.

"You be good while you're off at camp." She tried to make her voice sound light, but I could almost feel the tears behind her eyes. "Behave yourself. I don't want you to come home with any bad habits." She rubbed my head and stroked my back. "No smokin' or drinkin' or stuff like that. Understand?"

The sound of her voice made me want to wag my tail, but the sadness and worry that crept through her light tone kept my tail still.

Next thing I knew, we were in My Justin's machine monster. I got to sit in the middle. It was exciting. I watched the birds that flew by and tried to jump and get a better look at them. My Justin kept pushing me down and telling me to sit.

I was a little worried, too. But when we drove right past the building with the big gray blocks, I wasn't worried anymore. Where we were going or what we were going to do, I had no idea.

But like I said, my Mys loved me. They'd never do anything bad to me, so where we were going or what we were going to do . . . well, it really didn't matter.

Chapter 10

*O*ur machine monster roared and rumbled for a long, long time. I got tired of My Justin shoving me down when I tried to look out the windows, so I curled up in the seat and took a nap.

When the machine monster stopped, it woke me up. I sprang to my feet and looked around.

It was a strange place. Out the back of the machine monster, I could see a yellow house. There was no fence around it like at our house. Out My Justin's window, I could see a field. It was big and open—the perfect place for running and exploring and finding new smells. I was so excited, I could hardly wait. I tried to climb over My Justin to get out. He shoved me back. Then I looked out the front.

All of a sudden, my eyes got big. They must

have been as big around as Gray Cat's eyes were the first day he found me in his yard. The air caught in my throat and my tail quivered.

Dogs!

There were dogs everywhere! On my good-ear side, there were rows of small pens with cement floors and wire like around our backyard. On my hurt-ear side, was a huge brown barn. There were pens with dogs in there. Beyond were more rows of dogs. Big dogs. Huge, enormous dogs. Dogs with long hair and dogs with short hair. Some dogs looked like me. I'd never seen so many dogs.

Then My Justin opened the door.

The barking scared me to death. Some barks were happy. Most warned of a machine monster that had driven up. Others threatened—mean and scared and angry.

My Justin got out. My Bill got out.

The barking made me tremble. My Justin pulled on the rope, but I couldn't move. He pulled harder. I dug my toenails into the seat. I didn't want to get out—not here—not in this horrible, scary place.

"Come on, J.C.," he ordered. But when I wouldn't move, he picked me up and set me on the ground. I wanted to go back in the belly of the machine monster. I jumped for it, but he yanked my leather strap and slammed the door in my face before I could make it to safety.

I was terrified. The sounds, the smells . . . it was all so new—so strange and scary.

Suddenly, the barks from all the dogs sounded happy, almost excited. I peeked under the truck to see what was going on.

A man People walked from the house. I could see boots and blue jeans. Clinging close to the safety of My Justin's heels, I followed him behind the truck. The man had hair on his face. Sort of like dog hair, but he was still mostly naked. He touched paws with My Bill and they pumped their arms up and down.

"I do believe that pup's bigger and more developed than the rest of the litter," the man told My Bill. "He's one fine-lookin' pup."

He took the rope from My Justin's paw and began to pull.

"Hold it!" I screamed. "Wait a minute. I don't want to go with you. I want to stay with My Justin."

I locked my arms and dug my paws into the ground. He pulled harder. I fought him. I twisted my head and neck, trying to slip the leather strap over my ears. He dragged me around in front of the truck.

The dogs barked when they saw me. Finally, the man stopped pulling.

"Look at the little punk," a voice barked from one of the pens.

71

"Ah, he's nothin' but a stinkin' pup," another called.

"If he puts that pup in here, I'll eat him for supper."

"Come on, guys," a girl barked. "He's just a baby. Quit scaring him."

"Looks like supper to me," a deep voice roared. I felt the hair bristle on my back.

"You can't scare me," I growled, trying to sound brave. "I'll . . . I'm gonna . . . I'll . . ." I stammered, suddenly realizing that I was just too scared even to try and sound brave. "I want to go home!"

All the dogs barked their laughter.

My Justin and My Bill followed as the man dragged me to a row of pens. No matter how much I jumped and jerked or tried to hide behind My Justin, he just kept pulling. I couldn't get away. It was no use.

Before I could even yell "HELP!" he opened one of the pens, slipped the rope off my leather strap, shoved me inside, and closed the gate.

I lunged against the fence.

"Let me out! Please. Don't lock me in here!"

I lunged against the fence again. My Bill and My Justin were right there. They stood looking down at me. "Let me out," I begged. "I want to go home with you. Don't put me in here."

I stuck my nose against the very corner of the tiny pen. There I froze. I didn't move. My tail didn't quiver. I didn't blink. I didn't hardly breathe.

They watched me for a moment.

"Why are you doing this to me?" I wondered. But they didn't hear me—either that or they just didn't understand. "I've been a good boy. I haven't chewed up any shoes lately. And I didn't mean to pee on the floor yesterday. Was it my ear? Is that why you're doing this to me—because I ripped my ear and you don't think I'm pretty anymore?"

My Bill and the man with the fuzzy face went to talk with the dog in the pen next to me. My Justin reached through the fence and rubbed my nose.

"You be a good boy for Tommy," he said. Then he whispered: "I love you."

I stood frozen with my nose pressed into the corner of the cold steel pen.

"It's a lie," I answered without moving so much as a single muscle. "If you loved me, you wouldn't do this to me. What did I do? Why is this happening?"

Then, shoulders slumped and his bottom lip sticking out, he walked away. My Bill left the pen next to mine and paused beside me a moment. "Be a good boy, J.C." he said, trying to smile. He walked away, too.

From the very corner of the pen, I could see them standing behind the machine monster.

73

They talked for a long time. I couldn't hear their words. There was too much barking and growling all around me.

Maybe they were punishing me for something I had done. My Justin had hit me and talked to me real mean a couple of times. My Carol swatted my bottom and rubbed my nose on the wet spot I left on her carpet. Maybe it was something like that. Soon it would be okay. If they were punishing me, they would come back and get me and hug me and love me—everything would be all right again.

Sure enough . . .

When I saw My Bill come around the truck and walk toward where they left me, I was so happy I thought my tail was going to knock the whole pen down. I jumped up on the fence to greet him. My Bill touched my nose through the fence.

"You be a good boy for Tommy," he whispered. "We love you. You're only gonna be here a couple of months and we'll come back for you."

Then he turned and walked away.

"NO!" I begged. "Please don't leave me!"

He kept walking.

"Come back," I howled. "Don't go away. Please. Don't leave. Please, don't stop loving me!"

I stood for a long, long time with my paws on the fence. I didn't move. I didn't even breathe

deep. The big dogs who lived in the tiny pens that lined either side of the walk finally quit threatening me and quieted down. When my hind legs began to tremble, when My Justin and My Bill climbed into the machine monster and left, and when I finally realized they weren't coming back for me, I let go of the fence and stood with my nose against the gate.

The lights went off in the yellow People house. The dogs in the other pens curled up and went to sleep. All except for one. Someplace, from far at the other end of the pens, I heard a sound.

Old Blue howled.

It was a mournful sound. Soft and low, it crept through the darkness of our kennel that cool fall evening like a snake. The sadness of its cold hard coils wrapped around me, cutting off the last fading hope that my Mys, whom I trusted and whom I once thought loved me, would ever come back.

I pressed my ears flat against my head, trying to shut out his cry. Still it got through. It made my insides feel as cold and lonely as he was. It hurt.

Until Old Blue howled, I had no idea where I was. But when I heard his mournful cry, I remembered Mr. Tommy's kennel and Mother and my brothers and sisters. I remembered how special My Carol's look made me feel that first day I saw her and how wonderful her touch was. I remembered how excited I was when she put me in the machine monster and took me to her People house. I remembered how she loved me even when I threw up on the cloth seat of her machine monster. I remembered My Justin and how he let me sleep in his waterbed and how I felt safe and protected. I remembered My Bill who let me lie in his lap and how he talked to me and petted me.

With each memory, the hurt tightened around my heart.

How could my Mys be so cruel? How could they care for me and love me and make me trust them . . . then simply throw me away like an old piece of trash in this horrible and lonely place? How and why would they desert me and break my heart like they did?

I looked up at the half-moon, far away and cold in the black night sky. I took a deep breath. I closed my eyes.

I howled.

It was a mournful sound. Soft and low, it crept from my throat and through the darkness of our kennel that cool fall evening like a snake. The sadness of its cold hard coils wrapped around my heart.

I howled again.

Old Blue howled back.

The sounds were exactly the same.

Chapter 11

"**H**ey, kid. Knock it off!"

The deep growl startled me. My mouth snapped shut and I looked around.

"Huh? What?"

"I said, knock it off! It's hard enough to sleep with Old Blue howling. Now I gotta listen to you, too."

I cocked my ears and leaned forward, staring into the darkness. From the shadows of the pen next to mine, an enormous dog appeared. He strolled over to the fence between our pens. "Come here, kid. Let me get a sniff so we'll know what's going on."

Cautiously, I moved over to stand near him.

He was HUGE.

I felt my eyes get big and my ears perk up when

he walked over to sniff me. My tail kind of tucked under me, too. He towered above me and I stood like a statue when he smelled me.

People animals are kind of weird. When they meet another People, they don't really know them. They don't know whether they're nice or mean. They don't know whether they're going to hurt them or be friends with them. It takes Peoples forever to truly get to know another People.

Dogs know each other QUICK!

Just a few sniffs, a twitch of the ears, and a wag of the tail—that's all it takes for us to know each other. By the time the dog was through sniffing me, he knew I was named J.C. He knew I had three Mys, I slept inside on a waterbed, I didn't like the sharp needles at the vet place, I was nice, and I didn't want anything to hurt my nose—not ever again.

"Okay, kid," he said, leaning close to the silver fence. "Your turn."

I turned and stuck my nose through the little squares of the chain link to check him out.

Big Mike was a bird dog—just like me.

Well, not really. He was a grown-up bird dog. He had a long, pointy tail, just like me. He had a good nose, just like me. He was mostly white with brown spots on his ears and side. His brown spots were dark and mine were more lemon color—but still, his markings were kind of . . . just like me.

From his smells, he had told me that he once had a My, but the People wasn't happy with him, so he sent him back to Mr. Tommy's kennel. Big Mike loved to hunt birds called quail. He was big and tall and strong and he knew about everything there was to know.

Then he told me the very best thing of all.

"Mr. Tommy's training me so I'll be a better bird dog. Pretty soon, I think your Mr. Bill will come back and take both of us home."

All four feet gave a little hop, all at once. When he said that, I spun to face him.

"He'll come back?" I panted. "He'll take both of us home?"

Big Mike shrugged an ear. "Yep. At least I think so."

I pushed my nose clear through the chain link until it stuck and I couldn't get it to go any farther. "You mean they *didn't* desert me? They won't leave me here forever? I won't have to howl at night like Old Blue? You mean, they'll come back for me?"

"Of course, you dope." He wagged. "Couldn't you smell how much they love you when they told you good-bye? They hadn't even left and they already missed you and wanted you back home."

My tail stuck straight in the air and I jerked my nose out of the fence.

"Are you sure?"

"Sure, I'm sure!" He wagged. "You got it made, pup. I mean, any bird dog who gets to live inside a People house, sleep on a waterbed, and get to take baths in the People bath bowl—man, you got it made for sure. I bet even if you never pointed a bird in your life, they'd still love you."

"Would they be proud of me?"

He flipped his tail to the side and sat down.

"Well, that's another matter," he answered with a shrug of his ears. "Your My is proud of you when you point quail. That's about it. But that's what you're here for—to learn. Now shut up and get some sleep. We both got a lot of learning to do tomorrow."

With that, he turned and went inside the big barrel in the middle of his pen. I didn't like the barrel in my pen. It smelled of Fat Mary, the dog who had lived here last. She wasn't a happy dog. She loved to eat, but when she did she got so fat she could barely run. They didn't feed her as much as she wanted, so mostly she was mad and unhappy. The barrel smelled of that, so I slept on the cold, hard concrete floor of my pen.

I *made* myself go to sleep! Even with the scary noises that came from the other pens—even on the cold, hard ground instead of my waterbed, and even with Old Blue's howls that sent the chills up my spine—I made myself sleep. That's because the next day, I would start learning to be a bird dog. I would work hard. I would do everything that Mr. Tommy wanted me to. I would be the world's greatest bird dog and my Mys would be so proud of me!

I worked hard. I learned all there was to learn. I didn't yank on the rope too hard and flip myself over when we went to the field. When Mr. Tommy or Roberto would throw the squishy thing with the feathers in it and yell "Fetch," I would chase after it and bring it back to them. I didn't bite it too hard, and when they said "Give," I opened my mouth and let them have it. I didn't run back to the pen when Mr. Tommy made the loud BOOM with his big double-barrel boom-boom stick. (A dog called Sam did that all the time. It made Mr. Tommy very, VERY unhappy.)

And when I found a quail . . . they were easy to find because they had the most wonderfully delicious smell that ever came to my nose . . . anyway, when I found them, I would follow them real carefully, so they wouldn't fly away. When they stopped, I stopped. Then I pointed at them, just like a good bird dog is supposed to do.

The moon came full two times. The nights became cool and crisp and the days not so hot and long. And just like Big Mike had promised, my Mys finally came for us. I could hardly wait to show them how much I had learned. I could hardly wait to feel what Proud was.

When I saw my Mys, when I smelled them, my tail wagged so much that it shook me all over. It shook me so hard that even my ears flopped.

"I really am sorry," Mr. Tommy told them. "That's the risk you run when you buy a puppy instead of a fully grown dog who has already been trained."

My Bill looked down at me and sighed.

"Are you sure?"

"Afraid so." Mr. Tommy sighed back at him. "He's broke to the rope and collar. He's not gun-shy. He stops when I give the command. He knows how to fetch and give. He doesn't bust coveys or singles. It's just . . . well . . . I guess his nose doesn't work. He won't point birds."

"What do you mean, my nose doesn't work," I gasped. "My nose works great. I really protect it, too. What are you telling them?"

"Not even once?" My Justin asked.

"Not even once," Mr. Tommy answered. "A couple of times, he acted like he was on a point. I mean, he freezes—gets really still. Only, his head's down between his front paws and his ears are dangling on the ground. When I kick around

84

in front of him there's not a bird. Darndest thing I've ever seen. I could work with him longer, but I'm afraid it would just be a waste of your money. I really am sorry. I'll tell you what, though. If you want a dog who's already trained, I'll give you the money back you spent on training J.C. and see if I can find him a good home."

"Why are you lying to them like this?" My tail drooped and slipped between my hind legs. "I'm a great pointer. I point quail all the time. Why are you telling my Mys this?"

My Bill was not proud.

My Justin was sad.

My Carol was happy to see me. She loved me very much. But no scent of Proud came when she reached into my pen and scratched behind my ears.

For an instant everything was quiet. No birds chirped in the trees. No dogs barked. Through the stillness, no sound came to my ears. A sound came to my heart, though. The sound of Old Blue's cry.

Chapter 12

I got to go home. I got to live in the People house. I got to sleep in the waterbed with My Justin. I got to sit in My Bill's lap in the evening when he blew smoke from his nasty sticks. He petted me and loved me. My Carol gave me baths in the People bath bowl and loved me just like I'd never been gone. They all loved me, but they weren't proud.

Big Mike got to live in a pen behind the silver barn. Almost every day, when My Carol and My Justin came home from school, my Mys would go hunting. They put on bright orange caps and bright orange vests. They picked up their boom-boom sticks, got Big Mike out of his pen—but they left Chomps and me home.

I snapped at flies or slept in the sun. Sometimes, I could hear the bang from their boom-boom sticks in the fields. When I did, I would jump up on the gate and beg for them to let me go with them. Just once I wanted to show them what a great pointer I was.

When they came home, I could smell the quail. It was a deliciously wonderful smell. I could smell Proud when they would pet Big Mike and give him an extra helping of food before they put him in his pen.

More than anything in the world, I wanted to feel proud.

Snow came. Little sparkly, silver crystals fell from the sky. The nights got really cold. The snow went away but the nights and days stayed chilly.

My Carol didn't like the cold. She was a little afraid of the boom-boom sticks, too. I could smell it on her. Although her boom-boom stick wasn't as big as the ones My Justin and My Bill carried, she just didn't like them all that much. So she began to stay home with Chomps and me.

I would lie beside her on the People bed while she put little red marks on papers. The papers came from the place she called school. Each one had a special smell of a different People. Most People papers smelled good. One smelled mean and sneaky. A couple of times I smelled where one People copied the very same thing another

People had written. My Carol must have smelled it, too. It made her really mad and she made a big red X on the whole People paper.

When it was almost dark, My Bill and My Justin would come home. Sometimes they smelled happy and proud. They smelled of quail. Other times, I didn't smell the quail on them. I didn't smell much Happy or Proud, either.

I stayed in the People house and longed to hunt quail and to feel proud.

Then one day it finally happened.

My Bill and Justin took Big Mike and left in the machine monster. My Carol put her school stuff on the bed and took her school clothes off. With nothing to do, I plopped on the People bed to wait for her. Sometimes she patted me while she was making marks on her People papers. Chomps jumped on the bed and lay down beside me.

"You want to play?" I asked.

He just flopped over on his back and closed his eyes.

My Carol looked down at him and frowned. Then she stood in front of the shiny piece of glass. She patted her tummy and frowned even more.

"That's it!" She snapped. "Cold or not, I've *got* to get some exercise. Wouldn't hurt you either, Chomps. You guys want to go for a walk?"

The familiar words "go for a walk" perked my ears and made my tail drum on the bed. When I saw her putting on her "go for a walk" shoes, I jumped from the bed so fast I almost broke my neck.

I ran to the door and put my paws on it. I ran back and jumped on the bed. She was still getting dressed. I ran back to the door, back to the bed, and back to the door. It took forever before she was ready.

When she opened the gate, I raced ahead of My Carol and Chomps. Gray Cat had caught a rat near some trees by the road. It was a big rat and had put up a pretty good fight. No coyotes had been around in a week or two. The rabbit who lived under the brush pile had seen me coming and was hiding.

I stood on my hind legs and looked around. My Carol was already headed up the hill. I raced to get ahead of her, because good bird dogs are always supposed to hunt in front of their My. I caught her and raced ahead to check out the plum thicket where the road turned.

That's when I smelled the wonderfully delicious smell of . . .

Quail.

I froze. The scent locked my legs and my head and my tail—every single muscle in my body tensed.

I tested the air again. They were close. There was more than one. More than two. There were a whole bunch of them. Without moving so much as a whisker, my eyes darted about. I saw them.

The quail stood together in a circle in the center of the plum thicket. Their tail feathers touched in the center of the circle and they watched, outward, so they could fly away to escape. Too close to risk getting any nearer to them, I pointed. I held them. As long as I didn't move, they didn't fly or run away.

I heard the footsteps. My Carol and Chomps came closer and closer.

But they didn't stop. They kept going.

"No! Come back. Quail!"

My Carol kept walking. Farther and farther down the road. Suddenly, she stopped.

"Come on, J.C." she called. "Come on, boy."

I didn't move. I didn't even twitch.

"They're right here. I'm pointing at them. Please . . . please see them."

My Carol came back. "Chomps, what in the world is that stupid pup doing?"

Closer. Closer.

Only she went the wrong direction. I could hear her stomping around in the brush, kicking at the grass. But she was going the wrong way.

"No," I said. "Right here. Right where I'm pointing. Why can't you see them?"

"Come on, J.C." she ordered. "This is ridiculous. I need to finish my walk."

My Carol started to leave.

"Wait, I see them," Chomps barked. Then quick as a flash, he charged past me on his short little stubby legs. I didn't even have time to yell at him to stop.

He raced smack-dab for the quail, yapping and barking every step of the way.

They flew. There was a sound of their short wings drumming the air. Feathers knocked against limbs of the plum thicket as they fluttered and scattered in every direction. Chomps barked louder.

And above the sound of the flying quail and Chomps barking, I heard My Carol.

"Well, I'll be darned."

She didn't let me go after the quail. Instead, she kept calling and yelling at me. Reluctantly, I followed her back to the house.

I waited in the backyard. She put Chomps in the house. When she came out she had on her orange cap and her orange vest. My Carol didn't like the boom-boom stick. The thing kind of scared her. But she brought it with her—that's how much she loved me.

Chapter 13

It was after dark when My Justin, My Bill and Big Mike came home. I played tug-of-war with Chomps and Wiggie. As far as I was concerned, Chomps was my best friend. If he wanted to play, I would play. If he wanted to sleep, I would leave him alone. If he wanted to eat his food *and mine* both—that was great. Anything he wanted was fine, because without him My Carol might have never seen the birds in the first place. There was no way I could ever thank him enough.

My Bill and My Justin didn't smell of quail when they came in. They didn't smell of Happy, either. They put their boom-boom sticks in the box and locked the door, then came into the kitchen.

My Carol hugged My Bill.

"You boys have any luck?"

My Bill sighed and shook his head.

"Nope. Didn't see one single bird all afternoon." He sniffed at the thing on the stove. "What's for supper?"

My Justin came to the kitchen, too. I let Chomps have Wiggie, and I followed him.

"Smells good," he told My Carol. "What is it?"

My Carol smiled. Even from behind My Justin, I could feel the proud.

"Quail."

My Justin jerked. My Bill's eyes got sort of big around.

"Quail?" they both said at the same time.

My Carol nodded her head. Her Proud feeling was even stronger. My Bill folded his arms and stared at her. My Justin lifted the lid off the thing on the stove, just to be sure. Then they both tilted their heads to the side.

"How . . . when . . . where . . . ?" they both sputtered and stammered.

My Carol stuck a stick with a flat silver end on it into the hot thing. It sizzled when she turned the quail over. I could smell the deliciously sweet aroma. She acted busy with her cooking and pretended to ignore them.

"Somebody bring us some quail?" My Bill asked.

"No. I shot them."

My Justin and My Bill frowned at each other.

"Who went with you?" My Justin asked.

"Just me and J.C."

The Proud that came from her made my chest fill and my tail wag.

My Bill's mouth flopped open. My Justin's eyes crossed and he shook his head.

"No way!"

My Carol shrugged and put the lid back on the hot thing.

"J.C. pointed them and I shot them. It's as simple as that."

Gasps and questions and other mouth noises filled the kitchen. They were so loud and so close together it almost hurt my ears. My Carol wouldn't answer them.

"I can't tell you, I'll have to *show* you," was the only thing she said.

That night my Mys ate quail for supper. My Carol gave me two to eat, all by myself.

My Justin got up before the sun the next morning. I wanted to sleep, but since I didn't like sleeping alone, I followed him into the back room. He turned on the noise box with the pictures. While he watched cartoons, I slept on the couch.

I guess he wanted to go hunting. He kept pushing the button on the noise box until it was so loud I couldn't sleep. My Bill and My Carol finally got out of bed and came in with us. My Bill looked disgusted at him when he turned the noise box down, but I could tell he really wasn't.

My Mys put on their orange hats and orange vests. They unlocked the box and got their boom-boom sticks out. Then all of us went hunting.

I don't think I was ever so happy in my whole life. Finally . . . finally, I got to take my Mys hunting.

Back and forth, I raced in front of them as we walked. We were clear on the far corner of our farm before I found the quail. It was a different covey from the one My Carol and I played with yesterday. There were a lot of birds in this bunch.

I found where they had spent the night. I could hardly tell which way they went. I sniffed and worked and sniffed. Yes. This way. They stopped here to eat. The smell was stronger now. They got a drink here in the pond.

"This way," I told my Mys. "Follow me, they went this way."

The scent was much stronger now. Strong and wonderfully delicious and . . .

Then I saw them. They scurried through the tall grass in front of me. I froze, then followed them, one step at a time. Creeping, easing closer and closer and closer until suddenly they stopped.

Beneath the limb of a cedar tree, they gathered with their tail feathers touching in the center of their circle. They faced out, ready to fly away if

I came any nearer. I stopped and pointed them for my Mys.

"What's he doing?" My Justin asked.

"He's on point," My Carol answered.

"A point?" My Justin's voice made a gulping sound when he swallowed. "It looks like he's getting ready to do a somersault."

"Yeah," My Bill agreed. "He's got his front legs apart. The top of his head's almost touching the ground between them. If he put his head down another inch or so and leaned forward, he'd roll right over. What's he doing, pointing with his ears?"

"No, his tail!"

"His tail?" My Justin and My Bill gasped together. "Any bird dog I've ever seen points with his nose."

"J.C.'s not *any* bird dog. He's special," My Carol said. "Where the tip of his tail is pointing— that's where the birds are."

The Proud that came from My Carol almost made my tail wag. But if it did, I might scare the quail. I stood frozen, watching the birds between my legs and pointing at them with my tail until my Mys walked toward the cedar tree and scared them up.

The boom-boom sticks made their loud noises. One quail fell and the others flew away. Most landed in the tall grass down in a valley. Five more flew back near the pond. As soon as I knew

where they went, I raced to pick up the quail that fell when their sticks said *bang.*

I brought the bird back and gave it to My Carol, then I told them to follow me. I showed them where the singles were and pointed them for my Mys.

We had quail for supper that night.

"Darndest thing I ever saw in my life," My Bill said when he finished eating. "Bird dogs point with their nose—not their tail. I just can't figure it out."

My Justin agreed with him.

"I've got an idea," My Carol began. "I think it happened when he was a puppy."

"What happened?" My Bill asked.

"Well, remember when we first got him?"

"Yeah."

"Remember how Gray scratched him and Chomps bit him and then he got stung by the wasp and ended up in the pool?"

"Don't forget the bird who pecked me," I told her, only she didn't understand.

"His nose puffed up like a balloon," My Justin added.

My Carol nodded. "Well, the way I figure it, everything on the whole place went for that poor puppy's nose. My guess is that he decided he was gonna get that nose ripped clear off him if he didn't protect it. So when he finds quail, he tucks his head between his front paws and under his body so nothing can get at it. Then he points with his tail."

"You finally figured it out," I said with a wag of my tail. "Peoples are kind of slow, but you *finally* got it."

"That's the craziest thing I ever heard," My Bill scoffed. Then he looked at me and smiled. "But why he points with his tail instead of his nose . . . well, it doesn't matter. He's one heck of a bird dog."

My Bill sat on the couch and patted his legs. I wagged my tail again and hopped onto his lap. I was getting pretty big—almost grown—so my head draped over his lap on one side and my rear end draped over on the other.

My Justin and My Carol came to sit with us. With my head in her lap, My Carol scratched behind my ears and loved my face. My Justin sat close and put my rear end on his lap. He patted my rump and scratched the good place, right where the base of my tail starts. My Bill rubbed my tummy and patted my middle.

The aroma of the quail we had for supper lingered in the air. It was a wonderfully delicious smell. But Mother was right. It was only the *second best* smell there was. The Proud that came from my Mys was by far the *best!*

I knew that Big Mike and my Mys and I would go on lots of quail hunts. I knew that I would

100

always love my Mys and that they would always love me—no matter what. And I knew that never again would I make that horrible sound that crawls through the night like a snake. Never again would I hear myself cry the sound of Old Blue's howl.

About the Author

BILL WALLACE has had a number of dogs in his life, but none has "wormed" its way into his heart as quickly as J.C. A pointer pup, J.C. was born on April Fool's Day. While searching for a trained bird dog at a kennel in Oklahoma City, Bill and his son Justin (not to mention the dog trainer) were "shocked" when Bill's wife Carol spotted the puppy and decided they should take him home.

Excited and frightened, the puppy threw up in the car on the drive back to the family farm in Chickasha. Gray Cat scratched his nose, Chomps growled and snapped at him, and when the coyotes howled that night, J.C. crawled into Bill's lap and shivered.

J.C. now sleeps on the bed, swims in the pool, chases birds in the backyard, and "points" with his nose. He also curls up at Bill's feet and helps the author while he works on his books.

Bill Wallace's novels have won seventeen state awards and made the master lists in thirty states.

The BILL WALLACE Collection

WATCHDOG AND THE COYOTES

by BILL WALLACE

ILLUSTRATED BY DAVID SLONIM

For
Kristine and Bethany Whitener

Chapter 1

*T*he warm dry breeze that swept in from the desert felt good on my cold nose. It tingled the little hairs inside my ears and made them twitch and wiggle. My left paw dangled over the edge of my floor. I draped my right paw over it and rested my chin.

I watched.

The sun was nothing but a huge orange sliver above the wooden fence around the backyard. It was pretty, but I forced myself to quit thinking about it. I had to watch. That was my job—and I couldn't afford to mess up again. This was my third chance—probably my last.

In a moment the sun would disappear and the

1

only thing left would be a bright glow. Higher in the sky were mixtures of yellow and gold. Streaks of clouds were darker. Low in the sky, they were blue. Above, the blue changed to a deep purple. I wished the fence wasn't there. I wished—just once—I could see all of the sunset.

Far off in the desert a coyote howled. It was a lonely sound. It made me feel lonely, too.

I watched.

But behind my eyes, visions came. Memories flooded my mind. I missed my mama. She had been so big and wise. I missed my little boy. He had been fun and full of laughter. I missed my big boy. He was rough-and-tumble, and I could play with him and not have to worry about him crying. How I longed to be with them.

Not that I didn't love my new master. He was nice. His laugh rolled and tumbled through the air like thunder rumbling before a storm. But he was just too old to play. His wife didn't play with me, either. They fed me well. They petted me and scratched behind my ears. But there was no romp or play in either of them. That was what made me lonely, especially on nights like this, when they weren't home.

I watched.

After a time, the deep purple color filled the

sky. The smell of night came and all was quiet, and the quiet made me feel even more alone.

Things could have been worse, I guess. That's why it was so important for me to watch. That's why I had to do a good job. I had to be careful.

Scotty had warned me. Scotty was a Scottie. He had lived in the yard next to mine back when I lived in California. There had been a chain-link fence between our houses, and not only could we visit but we could actually see each other. Scotty told me that he was a digger.

"It's a bad habit," he'd explained. "I just can't quit digging. It's kind of like some masters have a habit of smoking cigarettes, and no matter how hard they try, they just can't break the habit. I'm like that, too. Only I don't smoke, I dig."

Scotty was on his third master when I met him. Two days after our last visit Scotty dug up the guy's rosebushes, and sure enough—straight to the pound.

That's it, man. About three masters is all a guy gets, then off to the pound.

Despite the warm breeze from the desert, the memory of Scotty sent a chill up my back. The Shaffers were my third masters.

A sound jerked me from my sad memories. I watched.

For a time there was nothing. Then a black stocking cap appeared above the back fence. It hesitated there a moment, then rose. I watched.

A man's face was under the hat. Nervous eyes scanned my yard. A wisp of the fall breeze brought a scent to my nose. Something about it was almost familiar, but it was a smell I didn't know, an odor that I couldn't taste or understand. The man looked all around. Then there was another clunk as his shoe found the wood rail and he climbed over the fence.

I watched.

Wonder why he didn't use the gate, I thought as he jumped from the top of the fence. When he landed, he looked all around again. He had on a black cap and a black shirt and black pants. The only part I could really see of him was his face. His eyes and forehead scrunched up when he looked toward my doghouse. The way he acted, the way he smelled—it brought a feeling from deep inside me. His actions made the hair bristle in a sharp ridge down my back. He inched forward. Watching him made my lip curl. My teeth felt dry. He stood very still for a moment, then edged toward the house.

I watched.

4

I guess he hadn't seen me where I rested inside my house. When he got close he suddenly froze, dead in his tracks. He started to shake all over.

"Nice doggy." His voice quivered when he whispered to me. "Nice puppy."

The smell was much stronger now. I still couldn't hear or see or understand it. I forced my lips closed so my teeth wouldn't show. I made the hair relax on my back. My tail made a thumping sound against the wooden floor of my house. He seemed to relax. Then, never taking his eyes off me, he moved toward the Shaffers' house.

I watched.

But when he disappeared around the side of my house, I climbed out. I peeked around the corner of the doghouse and saw him kneeling down at the back door. He took a tool out of his pocket and started wiggling the doorknob. I could hear a jingling sound, but I really couldn't see what he was doing. I moved closer to watch.

The man worked and worked. Finally he glanced around. When he saw me standing right next to him, a little squeal came from his throat. He jumped so hard he landed on his bottom beside the back door.

"Nice doggy." His voice shook as hard as he

did. "Don't bite me." He put his hands up in front of his face. "Nice doggy."

The strange odor was very strong. It came from the man in the stocking cap. The smell sort of hurt my nose, but at the same time it made me feel big and strong inside. It was weird!

"I won't bite you," I assured him. "I'm nice. I learned my lesson with my last master. I'll never bite anything or anybody ever again."

But, like most people, I guess he just didn't understand Dog. He kept his hands up and kept shaking for a long, long time. At last, when I kept wagging my tail and smiling at him, he crawled back to his knees and jiggled the doorknob some more.

I watched.

He opened the door and went into the Shaffers' house. I could hear him rattling around inside. Every now and then I could see the glow from the little light he held in his hand. After a while he came out the door.

I watched.

He carried a big sack to the back fence and lifted it over. Then, still shaking and smiling at me, he came back to the house.

I watched as he carried another bag to the back fence, then another. When he climbed over the last time, he waved at me.

6

"You dumb mutt. You're the kind of watchdog that I love."

I smiled back at him and waved good-bye with my tail. I didn't really like being called a dumb mutt, but the way he laughed and smiled made me feel good. In fact, I could hear him laughing and chuckling as he dragged the heavy bags all the way across the sandy field behind my yard. Besides, he did say that I was the kind of watchdog that he loved. That made me feel great.

More than anything else in the whole world, being a good watchdog was the one thing I wanted. I guess I'd done a good job, too. I knew my new master, Mr. Shaffer, would be very proud of me, because . . .

I watched—just like a good watchdog is supposed to.

Chapter 2

"**I**'m going straight to the pound," I whined. "This is it. There's nothing else left. I'm a goner."

I paced up and down by the fence along my side yard. I didn't know what the pound was like, but I remember Scotty whining and crying when his master was about to take him there. I remember that I never saw him again. Whatever the pound was, it was bad.

"This is it," I whimpered. "He's gone in to get my collar, and when he comes back out . . ."

My tail tucked under my belly. My floppy ears drooped so low they almost dragged on the ground.

"What are you whining about?"

9

I jerked. The growl from the other side of the fence startled me. My droopy ears perked up.

"Who's there?"

"What are you whining about?" the voice repeated. It was Red, the Irish setter who lived in the yard next to mine.

I'd never seen Red because of the wooden fence. In fact, this was the first time he'd ever talked to me in the whole two months since he had moved next door with his family. I'd tried to talk with him before, but he only snarled at me through the cracks between the fence boards.

It was good to hear another voice. Besides, I was in so much trouble that I really needed someone to talk to, even if it was someone who only growled.

I squinted, trying to see through one of the cracks.

"I messed up," I told the fence. "I messed up bad, and I don't even know how it happened."

Red hair and one white eyeball appeared at the crack.

"I saw the cars with the red and blue lights on top last night," Red said. "The men in the blue uniforms kept going in and out of the house, and your master kept yelling. What did you do, get inside and tear the living room up or something?"

"No!" I shook my head so hard my ears flopped against my cheeks. "I'm a watchdog. I don't go inside."

"So what did you do?"

"I did what I was supposed to do." I shrugged both ears. "I watched."

Red growled, "Exactly *what* did you watch?"

I folded my tail under my bottom and sat down. "Well," I began, staring at the eyeball. "Last night I was watching, just like I'm supposed to. A little while after dark, this man dressed all in black climbed over the back fence. He kept wiggling something at the door, and finally he went inside."

"What did you do?"

"I watched," I answered, wiggling my whiskers. "I watched him bring a big sack out of the house and lift it over the fence."

"Then what?"

"I watched him bring out two more sacks."

Red snorted. "And you watched, right?"

I smiled. "Right."

"That's all you did?"

I twitched my whiskers. "That's what I'm supposed to do. I watched because I'm a *watchdog*."

"You didn't growl or bark at him?"

"Oh, no. Dogs get in trouble for barking and growling."

"You didn't bite him?"

"Heaven forbid! I never bite. *Never!*"

There was a strange *whoompf* from the other side of the fence. I pressed my eye closer to the crack. Red had fallen on his side. He rolled back and forth. He wagged his tail and laughed and laughed and laughed.

"It's not funny," I whined. "I'm in trouble. My master's probably going to take me to . . . to . . . the pound."

Red just kept rolling and laughing. Finally he got to his feet and told me to follow him to the back corner of the yard. Once we got there he started digging.

"Dogs shouldn't dig," I warned him. "You'll get in trouble."

Red dug faster.

"No, I won't," he said. "The bushes are thick here. My master won't see the hole or the dirt. Even if he does, he won't get mad. Besides, you need help. You're the most confused, messed-up pup I've ever met."

My ears drooped, and my tail folded under my tummy. "Please don't dig. I had a friend named Scotty. He was a digger. His master took him to the pound. And when you go to the pound . . . well, no one ever comes back from the . . . the *pound!*"

Chapter 3

*T*he sand was soft. Within a few moments Red's nose appeared under the fence. More dirt flew and splattered the shrubs, and he had made a hole deep enough for him to squeeze through.

When he stood up on my side of the fence, he kind of grunted and stretched. "Man, I'm getting too old for all that hard work."

Red didn't look quite the way I had pictured him from my view through the crack in the fence. He wasn't nearly as tall as me, but he was still sleek and trim. He had long red hair, except for the tufts around his forehead and whiskers. There his coat was beginning to turn white with age.

13

He moaned again and wiggled so the sand would fall off his belly. After that, he sniffed me all over. Then he explored my yard and came back to sniff me again.

He folded his tail to the side and sat down on one hip. "Well," he announced after his inspection. "You're no coward. You're big, but you're just as gentle as you said you were." He cocked a red ear. "You're not stupid, either—but you sure are mixed up."

I tilted my head to the side. "You can tell all that from sniffing?"

"Listen, pup. When you get to be my age you learn to tell a lot about dogs—and people—from a good sniff."

A shudder made the hair on my back bristle as I looked at the hole Red had left under my fence. "We should hide," I whimpered. "I'm in trouble already. When my master sees the hole you made"—I swallowed and shook all over—"I'll probably get sent to the pound. I don't want you to get sent there, too."

"Every time you mention the pound, your smell of fear hurts my nose," Red snorted. "My master's not gonna send me to the pound."

"Are you sure?"

"Of course I'm sure." Red yawned. "Long time ago I was running in the pasture with him and his boy. We found this pond, and I jumped in. I love the water. Only thing Irish setters love more than running is swimming. Anyway, his boy—dumb kid—decides to jump in with me. Idiot didn't know how to swim.

"Well, he started flopping around and screaming, so I paddled over to see what his problem was. Little rascal latched on to my tail. Only thing for me to do was paddle for the bank. Either that or let the kid drown both of us. My master got there just as I was dragging his boy up on the bank. I guess he figured the kid fell in and I jumped in to save him—neither one of 'em was ever too bright. Anyway, since that day I've never had to worry about anything. I can dig in the dirt, I can wet on the carpet, I can even chew up the garden hose—he never gets mad at me. Thinks I'm the greatest dog that ever lived. So quit worrying about the hole. It's not a problem. You're the one with the problem."

I nodded and sat down on my haunches to face him.

"You're right," I sighed. "I really do have a problem. This is my third master. The other two got mad at me and gave me away. My friend Scotty told me that he was on his third master—but when his master got mad at him, he didn't give him away. He took him to the *pound*. Now

15

my master's mad at me and . . . and . . ." I sniffed. "And I don't even know what I did wrong."

Red flipped his tail to the side and rocked to his other hip.

"The guy you told me about, the one all dressed in black—that was a burglar. He must have taken things from your master's house. That's why all the cars with the red and blue lights showed up after your master got home. Why didn't you stop the guy?"

"How?"

Red cocked his ears and tilted his head. "Bite him, you dunce! Take a chunk out of his leg. Growl at him. Chase him off."

I fell to the ground and covered my head with my paws. "Oh, that's a terrible idea," I whimpered. "I can't bite. That's why my last master gave me away. I promised then that I'd never bite another living thing as long as I lived."

Remembering made me hurt inside. My tail tucked under. My head hung low, and my ears drooped so tight against the sides of my face that I couldn't even hear the desert wind.

Gently Red reached down with his nose and lifted one of my ears. "Calm down, pup," he soothed. "It can't be all that bad. Tell me about it. Start at the very beginning."

Chapter 4

When Red told me to start at the beginning, he probably didn't mean the *very* beginning. But that was when my problems had really started, so I told him about how I was the biggest puppy my mama had ever had. She told me that of her two litters, I was by far the greatest Great Dane ever. I guess that's why my brothers and sisters complained so much and why they called me a bully. When they shoved for the best sleeping spot, I shoved back. When they tried to muscle in for Mama's best milk, I wouldn't budge. Since I was so big, I always got what I wanted.

"When we played and wrestled and bit each other," I told Red, "even if I was trying to be gentle, they yapped and squealed because I bit too hard." With my paw, I brushed my whiskers. The memories made me so sad that even my whiskers drooped. "I didn't try to be mean. I was just big—it wasn't really my fault. But . . . well, it always hurt when they called me a bully, so I tried my very best not to hurt them when we played. I guess I should have figured out then that I was just too big to bite, even if it was only play-biting.

"Mama was the only one who really liked me. She used to look real proud when she said how big I was. Whenever I chased the sparrows away from her food bowl, she told me that someday I'd be a great watchdog."

I looked up at Red.

"That's what I've always wanted to be. As long as I can remember, I wanted to make my mama proud. I wanted to be a great watchdog. That's what I did last night. I watched."

Red lay down and rested his chin on his paws so he could look me straight in the eye. "To be a good watchdog, you got to do more than just *watch.* Now, I understand that your brothers and sisters calling you a bully hurt your feelings, but that doesn't explain the panic you went into when I asked why you didn't bite the burglar. There's got to be more to it than what you're telling me. The least you could have done is bark at him."

I covered my eyes with my paws. Red pushed them aside. "Tell me. Maybe talking about it will help."

The very thought was enough to make me whimper. I forced back the sound and tickled my whiskers with my long tongue.

"My first master was a little boy," I began. "Well, he wasn't a little boy, he was a *big* little boy. We lived in California, and he used to tie a red bandanna around my neck and take me to the beach. I'd run and romp, and when girls would pet me and say how big and nice I was, he'd come up and flirt with them. We had a good thing going.

"Only, like I said, he was a big little boy. I was still a puppy when he went away to this place called college. I missed him. I'd get so lonely I couldn't stand it. At night I'd cry and howl. The daddy didn't like that. He yelled at me. He even threw water on me. The neighbors had a cat. Sometimes the cat would come over and climb on our roof. Sometimes cars would park in the alley behind our house. Every time the cat climbed on our roof or the cars parked in the alley, I barked to warn the daddy what was going on. He never understood, though. Each time I

19

barked or howled, he'd yell at me or throw water on me. Even the neighbors yelled at me and threw stuff. They yelled at the daddy, too."

"People are kind of dumb animals," Red sighed. "They really can't communicate too well. So what happened next?"

"So," I continued, "one day this lady came to the house. I barked to tell the daddy that someone was there. She looked mean and acted funny. I growled at her, and she kicked me. Then she started pounding on the door. When the daddy didn't come, she started yanking on the doorknob and trying to get in. I was afraid she was going to hurt the daddy. So . . . so . . ."

"So?"

I sniffed. "So I bit her. I nipped her right on her big flabby bottom. I figured it would make her go away. Only she didn't go away. She started screaming and crying and yelling. The daddy came running out the door. He kept yelling at me and hitting me with a rolled-up magazine. He told me that if I ever bit his mother again, he'd take me straight to the pound." I looked at Red and swallowed the big knot that lumped up in my throat. "I didn't know she was his mama. I was just trying to protect him."

Red gave a little sigh. "It was an honest mistake. It really wasn't your fault."

20

"That's what I tried to tell him, only—"

"Yeah," Red knew what I was going to say. "Only he didn't understand Dog."

I nodded. "About a week after that, the daddy's brother came to visit from Oklahoma. He had a little little boy who came out and played with me in the backyard. He was real tiny, so I was careful not to knock him down and stuff. I really liked him, too. Anyway, the daddy told his brother that I needed a boy to play with, and since they lived on a farm in the country, my barking wouldn't bother the neighbors. He never mentioned that I had bitten his mother. The brother took me to live with them in Oklahoma."

Red rolled to his side and rested his cheek on the ground. "You bit somebody else when you got to Oklahoma, right?"

My ears twitched. "Well, no. Not really."

"You barked at stuff or you . . ."

Suddenly Red stopped and stared at the fence on the far side of my yard.

"Who's that?"

"That's Poky," I told him. "He and his master just moved into that new house two days ago."

"What is he?"

I shrugged. "Don't know. He won't talk to me. When I tried to make friends, he growled and told

21

me how big he was and how mean and terrible, and he said if he ever got ahold of me, he'd chew my head off."

"You ever see him?"

"No. The fence boards on that side are too close together. I can't see through them at all. But I know he's big and really mean. He told me so."

Red snorted. He made that grunting sound when he stood up. I followed him across the yard.

"Hi. My name's Red. I'm an Irish setter. This is my friend—"

"Get away from my yard!" The smell and the high, sharp growl from the other side of the fence warned us. "Back off or I'll rip both of you to shreds. I'm big and tough and mean."

Red's white eyebrows scrunched low on his red forehead. "You sound and smell like a beagle."

There was another growl from the far side of the fence. "Yeah, that's right. But I'm huge. I'm the biggest, meanest beagle you ever saw, and if you mess with me I'll—"

"Nobody's gonna mess with you," Red snorted. "I'm too old to fight, and this pup here is nothin' but a big pussycat."

"I'm not a pussycat," I pouted. "I'm a Great Dane."

"Some Great Dane," Red huffed. "You may

think you're a Great Dane. You may think you're a watchdog, but you act like a pussycat."

Through the fence, he explained to Poky what had happened with the burglar last night. Poky just growled at him. Red told him that he had dug a hole under my fence so we could be friends and he could help me. Poky only snarled.

Red confided in him that even though he was old, he still got lonely and figured it would be nice to have a friend. "Since I'm out making friends, I figure I might as well make friends with you, too."

"I don't want to make friends," Poky barked. "I'm too big and mean to have friends."

Red looked at me and winked. "We'll just see."

With that, he trotted to the corner where my back fence joined the side where Poky lived. My eyes flashed in terror as he started to dig. I was going to the pound for sure. Not only had I messed up and let the burglar in, but now there was going to be a huge hole in my backyard and I'd get blamed for it.

Chapter 5

"Please!" I whimpered. "Don't dig a hole in my yard. Mr. Shaffer will take me to the pound and . . ."

Red ignored me and kept digging.

I had to stop him. I remembered what had happened to Scotty. I couldn't let Red dig. In the twitch of a whisker, I leaped between him and the fence. I plopped down, right where he was digging.

He looked at me and snarled. Then, with a grunt, he pulled his paws out from under my bottom.

"Move, you big ox!" he growled.

Red tried to dig under my tail. I pushed my

bottom harder against the ground. "Please stop. If Mr. Shaffer finds a hole in his yard—"

"Get away from my yard," the high voice snarled from the far side of the tall fence.

Red moved around in front of me and started digging from a different angle. I put my front paws down and stopped him.

"I'm warning you!" Poky yapped. "I'm big and tough and mean and . . ."

Red moved again. He tried to wiggle himself between me and the fence so he could dig. I pushed against him and kept him from getting through. Instantly he scooted behind me and tried to dig there. He shoved, trying to make an opening between me and the fence. I pushed harder against the fence to block him.

There was a loud *crunch-crack!*

Something snapped. Something gave way. I felt myself falling. Paws and legs sprawling, I tumbled backwards. I landed on my head with a thud.

Suddenly I was no longer in my yard. I blinked and looked around. The fence was on the wrong side. I was on the wrong side! I was upside down!

From the corner of my eye I saw a white, black, and brown streak. It shot across the yard and disappeared into a small doghouse under a pecan tree.

26

Paws churning, I rolled from my back and struggled to my feet. Frantic, I looked all around.

"Where am I? What happened? Where's my yard and my food bowl?"

"Good job, pup!" Red's head appeared through an opening in the fence. Then his shoulders, chest, and rear. Finally his tail slipped through and he wagged it. "Wish I was big enough to snap boards like that. It would sure save a lot of time and effort digging under."

"What happened?" I repeated.

Red turned back to the fence. With his nose, he shoved on one of the boards. It swung from a loose nail at the top. As it moved, I could see the fresh wood at the bottom where it was cracked. The two boards next to it were broken as well, although I could barely see the crack. They were also held by one loose nail at the top of the fence.

"You snapped those three boards, pup. Just busted right through 'em. Those loose boards make a neat gate. The way they swing from those top nails—as soon as we go through, they just slip back in place. Our masters won't even know about it."

"But how do I get home?" One ear arched.

"Just stick your nose through the crack," Red explained. "Once you squeeze through, the fence

27

boards just swing back in place. I couldn't have done it better myself."

I stuck my nose in the crack. Sure enough the board moved over. I was so big that two boards moved when I thrust my whole head through. My yard was still there. So was my food bowl.

Just then someone nipped my tail. It was a gentle nip, more of a tug. I backed out of the opening and looked around.

Red tugged my tail again.

"Come on. Let's go check out the beagle."

I hesitated. The beagle, Poky, was big and mean and scary. I really didn't know whether we should try to find him or not.

Red trotted across the yard toward the little doghouse under the pecan tree. I waited a moment, then cautiously followed him.

"Why did you lie to me?" I asked.

The little dog cowered against the back wall of the tiny doghouse. He covered one eye with a big floppy ear. Poky was tiny. Well, I guess he was the normal size for a beagle, but compared to me he was tiny. He was mostly white with big black and brown spots on his fur. It would have taken five of him to make one of me, and he wasn't mean at all.

"Why did you lie?" I repeated. "You told me you were big and fierce and mean."

The floppy ear wiggled just a bit. I could see part of a soft brown eye.

"I could tell you were huge," Poky said sheepishly. "I was afraid if you knew how small I was, you'd eat me. So . . . well, I figured if you thought I was big and mean and tough, you'd stay on your own side of the fence. I really am tough, though. I'm a lot stronger and meaner than I look." Again, he hid his eye under his ear. "Please don't eat me."

Red plopped down on his bottom. He had to lean over to see inside the low doghouse. "Nobody's gonna eat you. We just want to be friends. Come on out."

Red and I talked to Poky for a long, long, long time before we finally got him out of his house. When he did come out, he tried to look mean. His curved tail stood straight up in the air. The hair rose along his back in a sharp ridge, and his little short legs were as stiff as the boards in the fence.

We all took turns sniffing and inspecting each other. Poky kept growling and telling us how ferocious he was. But he finally relaxed.

"I guess you guys are okay," he admitted. "You're just so darned big, though."

29

"I'm a Great Dane," I told him. "Great Danes are supposed to be big. We can't help it."

"I'm not all that big," Red confessed. "I'm really kind of skinny—mostly long red hair. Besides, like I told you through the fence, I'm too old to fight. And the pup here is nothing but a big ol' pussycat."

"I'm not a pussycat," I said. "I'm a dog. And I'm not a pup, either. I'm three and a half years old, so I'm an adult dog."

Red wiggled his nose from side to side. "Well, compared to me, you're a pup. I'm twelve. Besides, you act like a pup—won't even bite a burglar."

"A burglar!" Poky snarled. "Is that what all the commotion was last night? Man, if I ever get ahold of a burglar, I'll chew his leg off."

While we explored Poky's yard and peed on his shrubs, Red told him all about the burglar and why I didn't bite him because I made a mistake once and bit some old lady on the bottom. When the three of us squeezed through the boards to show Poky my yard and pee on my bushes, Red told him about how my brothers and sisters called me a bully and about how I was afraid to dig in the dirt because of this guy named Scotty who got sent to the pound.

We were just getting ready to crawl through

the hole so we could explore Red's yard when Poky stopped. His floppy ears perked up and his tail stopped wagging.

"That's my master's car. It's almost evening, and he's home from work." His tail made a circle. "My master will be out to feed me any minute now."

Red glanced at the orange sliver of sun that rested on the back fence. "We'd better get home before our masters find out we've been gone," he said. "First thing after they leave for work in the morning, we'll get together and see if we can straighten this pussycat—excuse me, Great Dane—we'll see if we can straighten him out."

Poky slipped through the opening on his side of the yard. As soon as his tail disappeared, the boards fell back into place as if they weren't even broken. Red made a grunting sound as he squeezed through the hole on his side of the yard.

"I figure you're safe," he called from the other side. "If your master was going to take you to the pound, he would have already done it, so quit worrying. See you in the morning, pup."

"My name's not pup," I told the fence. "It's Sweetie."

From the other side of the boards, I could hear Red chuckling.

Chapter 6

*T*hat night a coyote howled in the desert. He was much closer than the last time I'd heard him. The sound of his voice made me uneasy. His howl made the hair on my back stand on end. He was so close that I could almost understand what he was howling about—almost but not quite. The sound didn't make me feel lonely, though. Now, I had two new friends. Friends make you feel better.

I guess Red was right about my master. Mr. Shaffer didn't take me to the pound. In fact, the next morning he even petted me and scratched behind my ears when he put my dog food in my bowl. "Some watchdog you are," he said.

His words should have made my tail wag, but the way he said the word "watchdog" made my shoulders sag and my tail tuck under. I knew for sure that my master was not really proud of me. People are bad about that, I thought. They're bad about saying one thing when they really mean something else.

When Poky's master left for work, the beagle shoved the broken boards aside with his nose and came over to say good morning. We waited at the hole under Red's fence until we heard a door slam and a car pull out of the driveway. Then we went to visit Red.

Poky walked right through the hole under the fence. He hardly had to squat down. I couldn't get through. I was afraid to dig, so I waited by the fence until Red and Poky dug enough dirt out of the hole for me to squeeze my way under. We explored Red's yard and romped and even chased one another around and around the yard. Even though he was old, Red was still pretty fast. He got tired quickly, though, so we went to sit by his doghouse.

"Got plenty of food left," he panted. "You guys hungry? Help yourselves."

"I'm always hungry." Poky wagged his tail. "Thanks." Then he looked up at me. "How about you? You're as big as a horse. Probably takes a ton of dog food to fill you up. You go first."

I flipped my tail to the side and sat down. "I may look as big as a horse to you, but that doesn't mean I have to eat like one. I'm full. You eat. I'm not hungry."

Poky finished Red's leftovers. Then all three of us stretched out to soak up some of the warm sunshine.

We spent that day and the days that followed lying in the sun and playing chase. Red wouldn't run for very long because he got tired. Poky had lots more energy. He was quick, too. Just about the time I got to him, he'd dart to the side. My long legs were faster than his short stubby ones, but I couldn't turn as quickly. I nearly had to stop to make such sharp turns. Sometimes he'd turn so quickly that I'd stumble and land on my chin just trying to keep up with him.

I *did* have to be careful not to step on Poky. My paws were so big, and he was so small—one good smack might have smushed him.

I was glad that Red had forgotten to make me tell him about my little little boy. The memories of my boy and of Oklahoma always made me sad. I was having so much fun with my new friends. I wanted the good feelings to last, and I wanted to forget the sad times.

And we did have some wonderful times. We spent the fall romping and playing. We shared our food. We chased each other and lay in the yard to soak up the warm Arizona sun.

Winter tried to come a couple of times, but fall chased it away as quickly and easily as I used to chase the sparrows away from Mama's food bowl. I knew it would be that way, too.

The first year I lived with the Shaffers was in a place called Chickasha, Oklahoma. The winter there was cold and nasty. It rained, and a few times it snowed or the ground was slippery with ice. When the wind blew from the north, it howled! It shook the brown leaves from the trees and left them naked and shivering. It was a damp, cold wind that seemed to cut right through my fur and down to my very bones.

Then, two years ago, my master got a new job—it was called retirement. We moved here, to Scottsdale. Mr. and Mrs. Shaffer worked hard at retirement. She painted pictures, and he made things out of silver and pretty little blue stones. Each morning they got in their car and went to the shop. I didn't know what the shop was, but they always took their pictures and trinkets with them, and they always came home about the same time Poky's master did.

The two years we'd spent at Mr. Shaffer's new

job in Arizona had been great. The winters here seemed more like spring in Oklahoma. The wind didn't blow, and there was never ice on the ground to slip and fall on. I thought it would always be that way.

Only, this winter was different.

One night the wind howled. It was so cold that even the needles on the cactuses shivered. I kept hearing this strange sound, so I crawled out of my warm doghouse to investigate. The sound came from the direction of Red's yard. I leaned my ear against the wood fence and listened. It was a whining, whimpering sort of sound. It was Red's voice. It sounded as if he was hurt.

Quick as a flash, I darted under the fence and trotted to his doghouse. Red was huddled in the corner. He was asleep, but his legs shook and the whimpering sound kept coming from his half-open mouth.

"Red?"

He just trembled.

"Red," I said louder, "are you all right?"

One eye opened. He jerked, surprised to see my big head poked into his doghouse.

"What's wrong, Red? Are you hurt?"

"It's my arthritis," he moaned. "I didn't mean to wake you."

I cocked an ear and tilted my head to the side. "What's arthritis?"

He whined and straightened his front leg. "It's my joints. People get it, too. That's how I learned the word. My master is always moaning and complaining about his arthritis. It happens to us sometimes when we get old. Our joints get stiff, and they hurt. I guess the cold brought it on."

I nudged him with my nose. "I can help keep you warm," I said. I started to crawl through the doorway. Red's house wasn't nearly as big as mine. There wasn't room.

"Can you get up?"

Red moved his legs and groaned. I nudged him again. "Come on over to my house. There's plenty of room. We can snuggle up, and I'll help keep you warm. You won't hurt so much if you're warm."

It took the Irish setter a long time to get up. On stiff straight legs, he followed me to the hole under our fence. He let out a little yelp and moaned when he bent down to squeeze through. Once we were both in my house, I gave Red the spot I had already warmed up. Then I lay down and kind of made a curve around him so I could keep him warm. For a time, he moaned and whined. I snuggled closer, and after a while Red relaxed and fell asleep.

WATCHDOG AND THE COYOTES

Once I was sure he was warm and comfortable, I dozed, too. Tomorrow night, if it was still cold, I would invite Poky to come and sleep with us. It felt good to have a friend to snuggle up with. I don't think I ever slept so well. It was the best sleep I could ever remember.

Until . . .

Chapter 7

*T*he loud, awful sound of snarling and yapping and barking shook me from my sound sleep. I jumped when I heard the terrible noise. My head clunked the top of my doghouse.

I shook the pain away and frowned, wondering what all the noise was.

"What's going on?" Red moaned.

"Don't know. I'll go see."

I squeezed through the doorway of my doghouse and stretched.

"That's my bone!" Poky's angry voice came from the other side of the fence. "You leave it alone."

There was more snarling.

"That's my food bowl! You get away from it!"

Red poked his head out through my doorway. "What's going on over in Poky's yard?"

"Don't know." I shrugged my ears. "But Poky sounds very upset about something." I took a couple of steps toward the fence. "Poky? Poky, what's wrong?"

"Coyotes!"

"Coyotes?"

"Coyotes!" Poky screamed again. "You and Red get over here quick! There's a whole pack of them. It will take all three of us to fight them off."

Red tumbled out of my doghouse. He was so stiff and sore he could barely get to his feet.

"Come on," he yapped. "We have to help."

I followed him toward the broken boards.

Suddenly there was a loud growl from Poky's yard.

"Leave that alone! Get away from my food or I'm going to bite you."

"We're not scared of you," a strange voice snarled back. "If you bite us, we'll eat you up instead of just taking your food."

"I got friends," Poky barked. "You get out right now, or they'll come over here and eat *you* up."

The coyotes only laughed.

It took Red forever to limp across the yard.

He shoved the boards aside with his nose and stumbled through.

"Look!" a coyote yapped. "Another dog. He's big. Run!"

"Nah," another coyote scoffed. "Look at him. He's so old and crippled he ain't gonna bother us. Let's finish eating."

I reached for the board with my nose. I hesitated.

What if the coyotes didn't leave Poky alone? What if they tried to bite us? My legs shook. I couldn't bite them back if they bit me. I don't bite. Maybe I better not go through the hole.

But when I heard more snarling and growling followed by a sudden painful shriek from Poky, I shoved the boards aside and squeezed through the hole.

The coyotes scattered.

Three of them leaped over the back fence. But when the two others saw that I wasn't chasing them, they stopped. They crouched in the corners of the yard. They hid in the shadows.

I could hardly see them. But I did see their yellow eyes, which caught the light from the big moon. I saw how their white teeth shone, too. Drool glistened as it dripped from their snarling mouths. That was all I could see of them.

As I watched, I felt the hair rise in a ridge along

my back. Something from deep inside made my rage boil. Without knowing why, I trembled. That smell—the same one I had smelled from the man in the stocking cap—swept into my nostrils. It wiggled my nose, but at the same time the smell made me feel big and strong. My lip started to curl, and I bared my fangs.

Suddenly I caught myself. I was ashamed of the way I was acting. I took a deep breath and forced the hair to lie down on my back. I replaced the snarl on my lips with a smile.

Poky raced between Red and me. His legs were stiff. The hair stuck out in a sharp line down his back.

"Go get 'em, Sweetie! Go tear 'em up!"

I made the smile stay on my lips. I forced my tail to wag. "Is there a problem, here?" I asked calmly. "Is there something I can do to help?"

Poky snarled.

"Yeah, there's a problem. Those stinking coyotes are stealing my food. One of the guys that jumped over the fence took my best bone with him. Go get 'em, Sweetie. Eat 'em up!"

"Now, Poky," I soothed. "You know I don't bite. Let's see if we can talk this out. Let's try to be friends."

Poky's mouth flopped open. His head tilted to

one side, and an ear drooped so low it almost touched the ground.

"Friends!" he gasped. "With *coyotes?*"

"Of course," I nodded. "Friends are great. You can never have too many friends."

"But coyotes . . . !"

I ignored him and turned toward the yellow eyes and white fangs in the corner. "Hello. My name is Sweetie. I'd like to be your friend."

The coyote only growled. His yellow eyes squinted.

I shrugged. "I'm sure you know stealing is wrong. You didn't really mean to take Poky's food without his permission, did you?"

A very big coyote who was hiding in the far corner of Poky's yard took a step forward.

"It's been a very cold winter," he growled. "The rabbits are all gone. We can't find any lizards, and the people used a big machine to cover up all the garbage at the dump. We're hungry."

"Oh," I gasped, "that's terrible. I've never been hungry, but I'm sure it must be awful." I reached out a paw and laid it lightly on Poky's shoulder. "My friend here is a good dog. I'm sure if you had only told him that, he would have been glad to share his food with you."

"What?" Poky's eyes popped wide. "I can't believe you said that." He dropped his shoulder and

shook my paw off. "Share with thieving coyotes? You must be nuts!"

With that, he spun around. His nose in the air on one end and his tail in the air on the other, he trotted on stiff legs back to his doghouse. There he stood beside his food bowl and took a deep breath, trying to make himself look big.

"It's my food," he growled. "You know I always get hungry for a midnight snack. If they steal my food, I won't have any. I ain't sharin'. I'll fight for it before I let them steal any more."

My ears sagged. I heaved a deep sigh and sat down on my haunches. Red limped toward Poky. "Come on, Sweetie. Let's help the little guy."

I didn't follow him.

The big coyote took a step. I stood up. The coyote drew back his paw and trembled.

"Stealing is wrong!" I told the big coyote.

"No, it's not. It's the way we coyotes live. We take whatever we find. We get it any way we can. If we're smart enough and sneaky enough to take it, then it's ours. That ain't stealing."

I turned and shoved one of the boards aside in the fence.

"Then you can have some of my food. I don't have much left, but I will be glad to share it with you. That way we can be friends."

The coyotes only glared at me.

WATCHDOG AND THE COYOTES

After a long, long time, I finally gave up. If no one was willing to talk, the only thing for me to do was go home and get some sleep. I squeezed through the broken boards and curled up in my doghouse.

Things were quiet for a long time. Suddenly there was a little growl. Then: *"Yowieee!"*

I watched.

Poky shot through the broken boards with his tail tucked between his legs. Red limped after him. Poky raced across the yard and hid behind my doghouse. Red went through the hole and hid in his own house.

I crawled out of my house and went to see what was the matter.

"He bit me," Poky panted. "He bit me, and they stole the rest of my food and my chewy bone. Why didn't you help me?"

I leaned my cheek against the doghouse. "I tried. I offered to share my food with them."

Poky licked the little hole on his hind leg where the coyote had nipped him. "You can't share with coyotes," he snorted. "They don't know how to share. You give them a little bit and they take everything. You should have helped me."

His big brown eyes looked very sad. He stared

47

straight up at me and sniffed. "You should have helped me."

With that, he limped off and slipped through the broken boards. His head hung so low that his long, droopy ears dragged on the ground.

All alone, I crawled into my doghouse. I felt so sad and helpless that my ears dragged on the ground, too.

Chapter 8

*F*or the next three nights things were quiet and peaceful. Poky wouldn't talk to me. Red stayed pretty much to himself. He wouldn't come through the hole under the fence, and when I went to see him, he said the same thing Poky had: "You should have helped. I tried, but I'm too old and weak. They were going to bite me, too. You should have helped us."

Then he curled up in his house and wouldn't talk to me, either.

On the fourth night, the coyotes howled.

They were far off in the desert, but this time I could understand them. They howled about how hard life was and how they'd always been poor and hungry. They howled for the rabbits or any other animals to come out of their burrows. Because, as the coyotes put it, "You owe it to us! We won't hurt you. We'll just eat you. We *deserve* to be fed."

They howled about how there was no justice in the world and how unfair it was for dogs and cats and people and horses and sheep to have homes and barns to sleep in, while coyotes had to sleep in a hole in the ground.

And they howled and howled and howled.

The next night they came back. This time there were six of them.

Poky didn't try to fight them. Instead, he shot through the hole in the fence and hid behind my doghouse.

I went to Poky's yard to investigate. The big coyote with sharp white fangs met me.

I tried to talk with him. I offered to share my food with him. He only called me a big coward and told me to get lost.

It was a cold night. When the coyotes finished eating what was left of Poky's food, three of them curled up and went to sleep in his doghouse. I went back to my house and invited Poky to come inside and sleep with me. Poky didn't even answer. He stayed behind my house, pouting.

The coyotes came again the next night. This

time, they came right after dark. They got there before Poky had a chance to eat any of the food his master had set out for him. They spent the whole evening sleeping in his doghouse while Poky shivered in the cold.

They came back the next night, too. This time, instead of six, there were eight.

Three of them ate Poky's food and slept in his doghouse. The other five jumped over the back fence of Red's yard.

When Red called for help, Poky just thumped his tail on the ground. "He wouldn't help me," Poky huffed. "Said he was too old and sore. Darned if I'll help him."

"He *is* old, Poky. It's not his fault."

Poky just ignored me, so I went to see if there was anything I could do. I crouched down at the hole and stuck my head under the fence. Two coyotes stood there. One of them snapped at my nose. I jerked my head back. The coyote's teeth missed my snout by only inches. When I offered to share my food with them, they just laughed and called me a coward and told me to get lost.

Red tried to fight, but he was old and weak. It wasn't long before he came tearing under the fence.

"Why didn't you help me fight them?" he

asked, puffing and panting and all out of breath. "You should have helped."

Red went to the back of my doghouse. I followed, my ears dragging on the ground. Poky wouldn't have anything to do with Red or me. He slept in the middle of the yard.

After two days, my friends got hungry. We shared my food, and for three more nights the coyotes slept in Poky's and Red's houses and ate their food. They always came just after sundown and left before our people woke up in the morning. That way our masters never saw them.

One bowl of dog food wasn't much for three dogs. I ate very little. I didn't want my friends to be hungry. My insides felt empty. At night my tummy would growl. It growled so loud that it echoed in my doghouse and woke me. I didn't mind, though. I couldn't let my friends go hungry, and . . . I couldn't chase the coyotes away. I just couldn't bite.

The next night, the coyotes came back. This time there were ten.

Two coyotes went to Poky's yard. They ate his food and went to sleep in his house. Two went to Red's yard. They ate his food and slept in his house. The others crept through the holes on either side of my yard.

We had just started eating when they got there.

"He *is* big," one of the coyotes whispered as they crept closer to me.

"Yeah," answered the largest coyote, who I figured was the leader. "But he's nothing but a big coward. Come on."

Poky and Red tried to gobble down as much food as they could. They were very, very hungry. Bravely I turned to face the coyotes alone. I walked toward them.

"I am not a coward," I protested. "I don't bite because I want to be your friend."

The biggest coyote smiled. It looked more like a sneer. "See?" he told his friend. "What did I tell you?"

"Yeah," the smaller coyote said. "But he sure is big. I wonder how big he is?"

The leader pranced right up beside me. He told his friend to jump on his back. Standing, one on top of the other, the two coyotes came up to my shoulders.

I stood and watched them. "Why have you come? What do you want here?"

The coyote on top licked his lips. "Two bowls of dog food isn't enough for ten coyotes. We're still hungry. We want more."

While they were talking, the other four coyotes sneaked around behind me and chased Red and

Poky away from my bowl. The coyotes started to eat.

"I'm sorry you're hungry," I said. "But if you eat Red's food and Poky's food *and* my food, then what will we have to eat?"

"That's your problem." The coyote on bottom laughed.

"But we'll starve," I said.

"So?"

"So that's not right."

The coyote on top jumped down. "It's right for us. We take what we want. You dogs got a lot. You got plenty of food and nice houses to sleep in. We got nothin'. We want what *you* got. We deserve it."

"Deserve it? Why?"

The big coyote moved up beside me. With his shoulder, he shoved me out of the way.

"We've been poor for a long, long time—that's why! We eat rabbits and mice and lizards and berries. We even have to eat cactus sometimes, and garbage from the trash pile. We deserve better, and we're going to take it."

With that, he shoved me again. I staggered sideways and watched the two coyotes join their friends at my bowl.

For the next two nights we slept in my yard. The second night was terribly cold, and for the

first time in a long, long while we huddled together for warmth.

The coyotes ate our food. They gobbled it down and laughed. They slobbered and burped. Then they crawled into our warm, cozy doghouses and laughed and talked some more. All the while Poky, Red, and I lay shivering on the cold, cold ground. I never imagined things could get worse.

Chapter 9

The growling from our three empty tummies woke us early the next morning. Red struggled to his feet and tried to stretch. Sleeping on the cold ground made him stiffer than ever.

"We've got to do something," he whimpered. "We're gonna starve to death if we don't."

Poky got up and shook his curved tail. "What can we do? I'm too little. Sweetie won't even growl at a fly, much less bite one. You're too old and scared."

"Red's not scared," I protested. "He's a brave dog."

"He's scared," Poky repeated. "I smelled it."

Red slouched. He looked down at the ground,

and when he leaned forward, his long red ears covered his eyes.

"Poky's right, Sweetie. I am scared. When I was young, I didn't know enough to be scared. When I was older, I was strong and fast, and I'd chase dogs away from my yard. Even bigger dogs didn't scare me. It was *my* yard, and I wasn't afraid of anything. Now . . ." His tail slipped under his hip and curled around his tummy. "Now I'm afraid. I'm old and weak and sore. I know if I try to take on those coyotes, they'll hurt me. I hurt enough already, just from being old. I don't want to hurt any more. They might even kill me."

As he talked, that strange but familiar smell came to my nose. It hurt, but at the same time it made me feel big and strong inside. I tilted my head and cocked one ear.

"Is that what fear smells like?" I asked.

Red shrugged. "When you're afraid, you can't smell fear."

Poky sniffed at Red. "That's the smell of fear!"

I plopped on my bottom. I sat down so quickly I forgot to move my tail out of the way. It crooked under me, and I had to shift my weight to get it out.

"I smelled it before. I tasted it. Only I didn't know what it was." I glanced at Poky. "Why didn't I smell it on you the first night the coyotes came?"

Poky's tummy growled. "I was mad. When they stole my food, then got my chewy bone, I was so mad I couldn't even see straight. That was my favorite chewy bone. I was so mad I forgot to be scared."

I looked down at my front paws, remembering.

"I smelled something very close to it from the big coyote, the leader, only it went away. I remember because it was like the smell on the burglar that night he came to my master's house." As I stared down at my paws, pictures and smells and tastes flooded the space between my ears. "I remember tasting the smell on my friend Scotty when he left for the pound—only somehow it was a little different from the smell of fear on the coyote and the burglar. And I remember my second master. The little little boy and his . . . his father and . . ."

I stopped as the sadness swept through me and made me jerk.

Red turned to me. The white hair above his eyes wiggled. "You said you'd tell me about your second master." Red yawned. "Your little boy in Oklahoma?"

I had tried not to think about that. Having all the misery of putting up with the coyotes made me feel bad enough. Thinking about my last home would make it even worse. Talking would just bring the bad feelings back again. I didn't want to tell them, but Red and Poky kept insisting.

"I was only there for three or four months," I began. "My little boy was named Ben. He was real little—only about five or so in people years. With my big little boy in California, I could romp and play. We had a blast flirting with the big little girls on the beach. When we got home, my big little boy would wrestle with me. He'd roll on the ground and tumble over me, then he'd jump up and run. I'd chase him, and we'd romp and tumble some more.

"Things were different with my little little boy. I couldn't romp and play with him 'cause he was too easy to knock over. I'd follow him around, and he'd hug my neck and pet me. I'd lick him—real careful 'cause my tongue would send him flopping backwards if I kissed him too hard. He used to try to ride on my back. It didn't hurt much, since he was so little, but if I stood up, he'd fall off and start crying. I was always real gentle with him. I really loved him."

I sighed and scratched a flea that nibbled at my empty tummy. "Ben's mama had a dog—a poodle. Her name was Fu Fu. That poodle didn't like

Ben, she hated me, and she didn't like the mama too much." I licked my whiskers and flopped my ears. "Come to think of it, I don't suppose Fu Fu even liked Fu Fu.

"Mostly she stayed in the house. But one day she had an accident on the carpet. The mama shoved her out the door into the yard where Ben and I were playing. I was polite and said hi to her, but she just stuck her little nose up in the air. Ben wanted to play with her. But she just walked off with her nose held high and snooty. Ben followed her.

"He chased her all around the yard. She growled and told him to quit. I tried to explain that all he wanted to do was play, but she didn't care. 'I hate kids!' she growled. 'Get the little stinker away from me or I'll bite him.' I didn't believe her. I guess I should have."

As I remembered that terrible day, a tear rolled from my eye. I wiped it away with a paw.

"Finally Ben cornered Fu Fu at the back of the yard. He kept trying to pet her and pick her up. I told him to stop. I tried to get him to play with me, instead. I tried to warn him, but . . ." I took a deep breath, sighed. "But he didn't understand. When he tried to pick Fu Fu up, she bit his hand. He jumped back, and Fu Fu bit him on the leg.

When Ben ran away, she chased him. She kept biting at him, and she got ahold of his leg again.

"That made me mad. I mean, she'd already chased him away. He was crying and hurt, but she just kept snapping and snarling and biting. I ran after them. I told her to leave my Ben alone, but she bit him again. He fell down and started crying really loud. I had to make her stop! I couldn't let her hurt my little boy. So . . . so . . . I bit her.

"I didn't mean to bite her hard. I just wanted to make her stop hurting my boy. But . . . well, she was little and I was big. When I picked her up, Fu Fu screamed. I threw her across the yard. She didn't get up, at first. She just whined and squirmed around on the ground.

"Fu Fu finally got to her feet, but she could barely walk. She limped and cried as if I'd half killed her. I didn't mean to bite her. I didn't think I had really hurt her. I just wanted to get her away from my boy. But I was mad and . . . and . . . my Ben was still crying, and a little blood leaked from a hole on his leg where Fu Fu had nipped him. I nuzzled him with my nose. I kissed him with my tongue, but he kept crying. I was afraid he might be really hurt, so I picked him up and took him to the house, and . . . and then . . ."

I couldn't finish. I was shaking all over.

"Let me guess," Red snorted. "Ben's father came out to see what all the crying was about. He saw Fu Fu lying in the yard and saw his boy dangling from your mouth."

I nodded, feeling my tail begin to tuck itself under my tummy.

"When you tried to explain that you'd saved your boy from Fu Fu, the father wouldn't listen, right?"

I nodded again and flattened my ears against my head. "I guess he thought I had attacked Fu Fu, then turned on Ben. I guess he didn't know I was bringing Ben to his daddy. He must have thought I had bitten Ben, too.

"I'd never bite my boy. I loved him. I'd never do anything to hurt him. But that's when I smelled it—the fear. I'd never smelled it before— that was the first time. It was a little different from the smell of that burglar and the smell from the coyotes, but very close. The smell jumped from the daddy so strong that I could taste it, even with Ben in my mouth. He took Ben away from me and kicked me. Right on the side of my head. That spot still hurts. I can feel it now, just as if it happened yesterday instead of a long time ago."

I flopped down on the ground and covered my

face with my ears and paws. I felt so rotten and sad that I almost made myself sick. My tail was tucked under me so tightly that I couldn't even feel it. My nose, which was always cold and damp, felt as hot and dry as a bone that had been left in the sun. I wanted to curl up and die.

Chapter 10

Poky and Red tried to comfort me. They nuzzled me with their noses. They licked my ears and nudged me with their paws. They talked to me and rubbed their cheeks against my forehead.

"You did the right thing," Red told me. "The poodle was hurting your boy. You had to make her stop."

"I didn't mean to hurt her," I sniffed. "She never could walk very well after that. They had to take her to the vet and . . . and . . . after she came home, she still limped." I sighed and let my ears droop over my eyes. "Fu Fu always limped."

"It wasn't your fault," Poky whispered in my ear. "Fu Fu's limp wasn't your fault, and the

66

daddy getting scared wasn't your fault, either. He shouldn't have kicked you."

"Why couldn't I make him understand?" I whined.

Red grunted when he stumbled to his feet. "People can't understand dip," he snorted. "I heard that they *could* understand a long, long time ago. Then they learned this thing they call language—you know, the words they use. Ever since they got words, that's the only way they can talk. We use wiggles of our ears and our tails. We smell, we taste, we look. They forgot how to smell and taste and look. If they can't talk with words, they can't understand a stinking thing. I tried to tell my master about the coyotes. Idiot just looked at me and patted my head. You can wiggle your ears and give off your smells and twitch your hair till you're blue in the face. Without words, people can't understand diddly-squat."

Poky stood up and looked toward the back fence. It was getting late. "What *are* we going to do about the coyotes?"

My tail didn't wag, but at least I could feel it again. Red shoved me hard with his snout. I got to my feet. My nose was still hot and my insides shook, but I took a deep breath and cocked my ears away from my head so I could hear Red.

"Sweetie," he said. His eyes and ears spoke

very seriously. "You're going to have to do something. Poky is too little, and I'm too old. You're going to have to fight the coyotes. We can help, but we can't do it without you."

I shook my head. My ears popped against my cheeks. "I can't fight. I can't bite!"

"Why?" Red snarled. "Because you made a mistake once and bit some old lady on the bottom?"

"No. Because of what I did to Fu Fu and to Ben."

"You didn't do anything to your Ben. You helped him, and the dumb daddy just didn't understand."

"But what about Fu Fu?"

"She deserved it."

"Oh, no." I cringed. "She didn't deserve to limp for the rest of her life."

Red put one paw over the other and squinted at me. "You might not have even hurt her. She sounds like the kind of dog who just might be faking her limp to make the mama feel sorry for her and not throw her outside when she messes on the floor. Even if you really did hurt her, which I doubt, you didn't mean to. What would have happened if you hadn't done something?"

I shrugged my ear.

"What would have happened?" he repeated.

"Well, I guess she would have kept biting my boy."

"Right."

"She would have kept hurting him."

Red gave a knowing nod. "You did what you had to do to protect your master. You're still hung up about your brothers and sisters calling you a bully. You don't growl or bite because you're big and you figure you might hurt somebody. But if you hadn't stopped Fu Fu, she would have hurt Ben even worse. When you fight to protect your master, you're not being a bully. You have to do what's right."

Red grunted as he got to his feet. He stood in front of me—so close that his nose touched mine.

"You're scared that you might get sent to the pound. But even if it's dangerous—even if your people might not understand—you still have to do what's right. Doing the right thing isn't easy, sometimes. But if you don't do anything, if you just think being a good watchdog means doing nothing but sitting and watching . . . well, you still got in trouble with your master, remember. It's much better to do what's right, even if you get in trouble, than to do nothing at all.

"You have to help Poky and me with the coyotes. Protecting your friends isn't nearly as important as protecting your master, but we need you. We can't do it alone."

Red's words made sense. He took his nose away from mine and sat down. When he did, he groaned again. Red was old and feeble because of his arthritis, but he was wise. Very wise. Still . . .

I plopped down on my bottom and crunched my tail again. I didn't even move it, though. I just sat on it.

"I'm so confused," I confessed. "When I was a puppy, I was confused all the time. But I thought that when I grew up I'd know things. I wouldn't be confused. Only . . . now I'm grown up, and I still don't know . . ."

"What are you confused about?" Poky asked with a wag of his tail.

"Well . . ." I felt my cheeks puff out when I sighed. "When I smelled fear on the burglar, I should have chased him off. Right?"

"Right."

"And when I smelled fear on the coyotes, I should have bitten them, right?"

"Right."

"But I smelled fear on Ben's daddy and on my friend Scotty when he was headed for the pound, and I smell it on Red when he thinks about the coyotes. Am I supposed to bite them, too?"

Red stood up again. "No. It's a different smell.

Different kinds of fear have separate smells. They're very close, but different. One odor is simple. Your Ben's father was afraid you had hurt his boy or would hurt him. Scotty was afraid of the pound, and I'm afraid of the coyotes.

"The other smell—the one from the burglar and the coyotes—their smell is because they're scared of getting caught doing something they're not supposed to. The burglar knows it's wrong to steal, and the coyotes know it's wrong to take our food. It's still a fear smell, but it's sort of a sneaky smell, too. It's hard for people and animals to be brave when they know they're doing something that's not right."

I nodded, remembering how the smells were the same, only different. "Why does the smell of fear hurt my nose and at the same time make me feel big and strong inside?"

"A long, long time ago, before we befriended people, we dogs had to take care of ourselves," Red explained. "There were animals we could eat and animals that would eat us. All fear smelled the same back then. Life was much simpler. When we ran across something that smelled of fear, our bodies told us to chase it so we could eat. That's where the strong feeling comes from. But when people came . . . well, we like people, and we don't want to eat them. But sometimes they smell of fear, too. Most of us have learned to overcome our instincts and not chase them."

"I think I understand now." I smiled. "One kind of fear—when people are afraid of us because they don't know us or because we're big—we leave them alone. The other kind of fear—the sneaky kind—that's when we chase and bite."

Red's white hair at the side of his mouth curled to a smile. "Right."

Poky's brown eyes opened wide. "Then you'll help us with the coyotes?"

"Yes."

The coyotes didn't come when they usually did. I guess it was because Poky's master worked outside in the yard until after dark. He was piling hay and straw around his roses and cactuses because of the cold.

I ate every bit of my food. It felt good to have a full tummy. As soon as Poky's master went inside, Poky and Red came to my yard. It was cold, but we were full and cozy. We curled up in the spot at the middle of my yard where we had been sleeping. I don't know why we didn't go into my house. I guess we were just used to the low spot in my yard.

It was a lot easier to sleep, now that my belly was full and now that I wasn't confused anymore.

WATCHDOG AND THE COYOTES

How long I slept I didn't know. But in the very middle of the night Poky lifted my ear with his nose.

"I think we're in big trouble," Poky whispered. With his paw he nudged Red. "Wake up, Red. This looks really bad!"

Chapter 11

*T*here were twelve coyotes in my yard. While we slept, they had formed a circle around us. When Poky woke me, I saw the coyotes watching us with their yellow eyes. They licked their lips.

"We're hungry!" The leader drooled.

Still half asleep, I struggled to my feet. Our tummies were full, but we were still cold and weak from hunger. "We have no more food," I said. "You've eaten it all."

"So?" one scoffed. "You guys look pretty tasty to us."

"Yeah," another added. "I bet that little one there—the one with the big ears and long tail—I bet he's downright yummy."

They all laughed. It was an evil-sounding laugh. Yellow eyes shining, white fangs glowing in the night, they took a step closer.

"Get 'em, Sweetie!" Poky whispered.

I leaned close to his floppy ear. "Let's try, just once more, to be friends."

Poky rolled his soft brown eyes.

I turned to face the coyotes. "If you eat us," I reasoned, "there will be no more food. Without us, our masters will quit filling the bowls. Then you will have nothing. Nothing at all."

"We're hungry, now."

The circle of coyotes tightened.

"That big one ought to feed six or seven of us," one coyote yapped.

"I want a leg," another chuckled.

"I want his guts," yapped another.

I took a deep breath. I didn't want to bite. But I was not a coward. I took a brave step toward the coyotes. "Take me," I said, "but please don't eat my friends."

The big coyote, who always seemed to do most of the talking, grinned. "That's what we're planning to do."

"Yeah," another coyote snickered. "And when we get through with you, we'll eat those other scrawny mutts, too."

They all laughed and took another step closer.

Red backed his rump against me. He bared his teeth and growled. "There are some animals you just can't reason with. We've either got to fight or die."

Poky leaned against my leg from the other direction. "Ready to get 'em, Sweetie?"

"I'm ready," I whispered.

I felt the hair ridge-up along my back. I bared my teeth. Growled.

Only it had been so long since I'd growled that just a little "fruff" came out.

I took a deep breath so I could bark at the mean coyotes.

Only it had been so long since I'd barked that all I said was "yap."

The coyotes howled and laughed. One jumped in and nipped me on the leg. It hurt. I tried to bite him back. Only it had been so long since I'd bitten, my jaws didn't open. My cheeks just puffed in and out, making a little popping sound.

The leader of the coyotes jumped on Red. The Irish setter fought bravely, but in no time at all, two other coyotes had helped the leader knock him down. One chomped down hard on Red's leg.

Poky fought and snapped, but he wasn't very big. Two coyotes grabbed him. One holding each of Poky's hind legs, they stretched him out and started dragging him off across the yard.

Five pounced on me. Their sharp teeth hurt. I growled, but it was a soft, weak sound. I bit, but my jaws were so gentle that my teeth wouldn't have hurt a kitten. All I could do was stand there as they bit and slashed at me with their glistening white fangs.

I screamed with the pain. I hoped and prayed it would be over soon.

Chapter 12

Light flooded the yard.

"What's all the racket? Get out of here!" My master screamed as he threw open the back door. "Get away from there, you stinkin' coyotes."

In a blink of an eye, the coyotes scattered. A couple ran for the holes on either side of the yard. Most jumped the back fence and went slinking off into the desert.

As the three of us lay panting and whimpering in the yard, my master went back inside and got a flashlight. I could tell that he wondered what Poky and Red were doing in my yard. He didn't ask. Instead, when he came out again, he checked to see how bad our injuries were. Poky, Red, and

79

I each licked his hand and thanked him for saving our lives.

We were bleeding and hurt, but our wounds were not serious. My master went back inside his house. Poky, Red, and I huddled in my big doghouse and licked our wounds.

"They'll be back," Poky said. "We don't stand a chance."

I licked the cut on my paw. "We *do* stand a chance," I assured my friend. "My master scared them. He will watch to make sure they don't come back."

Red sniffed. He had a big cut on his nose where one of the coyotes had sunk his fangs in. "He won't watch forever. When the coyotes think it's safe, and when your master's no longer watching for them, they'll come back. Next time there may be even more coyotes. Your master may not always be here to protect us."

I licked my paw again. "Then we must learn to protect ourselves," I said. "It's been so long since I have barked or bitten that I've forgotten how. Tomorrow we go into training."

"What's training?" Poky whimpered as he tried to lick the cut on his neck.

"We're gonna get in shape. My first master in California used to run and lift weights and do exercises. It was to make him look pretty for the big little girls, but it also made him stronger. That's what we're going to do."

Before our masters woke in the morning, Red and Poky went back to their yards. They dug two new holes, right in the center of the yard by the fence. Sure enough, when my master told their masters about Red and Poky being in my yard last night, they came to investigate.

Since the new holes were in plain sight, they used shovels to put the dirt back. They never bothered to look for the other hole on Red's side of the fence or the broken boards at the back of Poky's yard.

As soon as they left, I started our training.

Since the coyotes had stolen all our bones, I sent Poky for supplies. His master's son had left a softball, a bat, and a basketball in the yard.

Poky's hind legs were stiff because the coyotes had tried to make a wishbone out of him, but he brought the things back to my yard.

Red and I took turns biting and gnawing on the baseball bat. Poky chewed the softball. Picking it up in his mouth, he would bite down as hard as he could. Then he would shake it and throw it high in the air. The second it landed, he would chase after it and bite it again.

I chased the basketball. I tried to bite it, but it

was just a little too big for me to get my mouth around. I chased it, nonetheless. I tried to pin it against the corner of the fence, and if it got away from me, I chased it some more.

Each night we slept in my doghouse. Each evening, before bed, we practiced our growling and snarling. We took turns snapping at each other, too. We wouldn't snap hard, but it was good practice at moving our nose or paw before it got bitten.

At first light we tumbled out of the doghouse. We ran twenty laps, one behind the other, around my big backyard. After biting practice, we played chase.

Red grumped and complained about his arthritis. He didn't like all the running, but he knew he needed to get in shape. With each day that passed, he could run longer and farther before he got tired.

Poky wasn't as fast as Red and I were. He was quick, though. Just as one of us would close in on him during the chase game, he would dodge to the side or double back. My big, long legs carried me so fast that once I stepped on him. Gamely, the beagle jumped up and shook himself. Then he and Red chased me.

A week passed, and no coyotes.

All three of us felt much better. Without the

coyotes, there was plenty of food. Our tummies were full. Our wounds had healed. We felt stronger with the passing of each day.

Then, late one night, the coyotes howled in the desert.

Poky trembled. He scooted closer against my side in my doghouse. "I knew they'd be back."

Red raised his head. "Maybe we should go out and bark at them. We could tell them how strong we are now. We could warn them not to come back. If we do that, maybe they won't bother us."

I didn't answer him. My tail made a thumping sound on the floor of my doghouse.

"They are way off in the desert," Poky said, still shoving himself against my side. "They probably won't come until tomorrow night."

The next day, it was training as usual. Red didn't grump about running laps. Poky bit the ball harder than he ever had before. I chased the big basketball around and around and around. If I could just . . .

Blamb!

Poky and Red were getting a drink. Both wheeled around.

With a smug grin on my face, I came trotting

toward them. A limp, flat basketball hung from my mouth. I dropped it at my friends' feet.

"I think we're ready," I said.

That night the coyotes howled again. My master and his wife drove away in their car. Where they went, I didn't know. I did know there was no one to keep watch. There was no one to turn on the light. There was no one to protect us but *us*.

A little after dark we heard the coyotes jump over the fence into Poky's yard. They laughed and burped as they ate his food.

"Shouldn't we go get 'em?" Poky asked.

I didn't answer.

A nose poked through the broken boards in the fence. The coyote sneered and looked around. I lay in the opening of my doghouse, resting my chin on my paws. The coyote disappeared, and we could hear them jumping the back fence into Red's yard.

When I heard them munching on the table scraps and the bones, I turned to Red. "Now," I whispered.

Red climbed over me and raced across the yard. He hid in the dark behind one of the shrubs. I turned to Poky.

"Now."

Poky started to climb over me, but then he stopped. "You're not going to try to reason with them again, are you? You do remember how to bite?"

I smiled. *"Now,"* I repeated.

Poky trotted quietly across the yard and hid in the dark by his fence.

After a while, when the coyotes were through joking and laughing and burping and slobbering, one appeared at the hole under the fence.

He saw me lying in the doghouse. He sneered and slipped through the fence. Another followed.

One, two, three, four, five, six, seven . . . Twelve coyotes slipped through the opening.

I crawled out of my doghouse. The coyotes came up and formed a circle around me.

"Where are your buddies?" The big leader licked his lips.

I didn't answer.

"It don't matter," he scoffed. "We'll just eat this one first. Then we can find the other two. They're probably hiding in the doghouse."

I forced the ridge of hair on my back to stay down. I didn't let my lip curl or my white teeth show.

"Wouldn't you rather be friends, Mr. Coyote?"

All the coyotes laughed and yapped. "Sure," one said. "We'll be friends."

"Yeah," another added, "just as soon as we're through eating you, we'll be the best of friends."

The big coyote trotted right up in my face. He snarled at me and showed his long fangs. "Why don't you just lie down, big boy? Make it a little easier on us." His nose was almost touching mine.

"Well, Mr. Coyote," I said softly. "If you don't want to be friends. Then . . ."

The big coyote's eyes flashed wide. All he could see was the empty cavern of my throat when I opened my mouth. I bit down as hard as I could.

The coyote's whole head was inside my huge jaws. When I let go, the coyote fell backwards. He tumbled over himself a couple of times. He landed on his back with his feet flopping in the air. Dazed, he finally managed to crawl to his feet.

His eyes rolled around in his face. He shook his head. Slobbers went flying all over the other coyotes.

"Did you see that?" he gasped. "He almost bit my head off." His eyes rolled again. "Man, talk about a headache!"

I took a deep breath and in my loudest roar I screamed:

"Charge!"

Chapter 13

*B*efore the other coyotes knew what was happening, I flew into them. Poky and Red charged, growling and snarling, out of the dark shadows at the corners of my yard.

Red knocked one coyote down. The coyote rolled about three times from the force of Red's powerful legs. Then Red bit another coyote on the back. Poky leaped at the coyote nearest him. Poky was small, but he did give the coyote a terrible bite, right on his soft tummy. The coyote squalled and fell over on his side.

With my mighty jaws I bit one, then another. With my big paws, I clunked a coyote on top of the head. I hit him with such force that the coyote fell spread-eagled to the ground and bumped his chin in the dirt.

A coyote lunged for Poky. Just as he had practiced in the chase game, Poky dodged out of the way. Before the coyote could turn, the beagle circled around behind him and chomped down on the coyote's leg. Squealing at the top of his lungs, the coyote raced across the yard, dragging Poky behind him.

One coyote jumped the fence. Then another and another.

Red chased one, snapping at his rump every step of the way. The coyote tried to jump the fence. But he was trying so hard to get away from Red's fierce jaws that he jumped a bit too soon. He didn't quite make it.

There was a loud crack as the coyote's head slammed into the fence. It broke a chunk of wood out. The coyote bounced off the fence and went flying backwards over Red. Before he could scramble to his feet, the Irish setter bit him once on the ear and once, really hard, on the nose. Running for his life, the coyote had to circle the yard again before he could get up enough speed to jump the fence. He made it this time. But he was in such a hurry that he scraped his tummy on the fence and left a whole bunch of hair stuck to the boards.

Through the broken-off chunk in the fence, I could see him. Tail tucked between his legs, he slinked off into the desert.

Suddenly all was quiet.

Red turned to help his friends. Poky was nowhere in sight and I didn't need any help.

Only one coyote was left—the big one who usually did all the talking. He lay in the middle of the yard. I stood over him, smiling. With my big paws, I pinned him to the ground.

"Please let me up," the coyote whined. "Please don't hurt me. Please let me go."

I ignored him. When Red came trotting over, I winked. "What do you think we should do with this coyote?"

Red winked back at me.

"Let's eat him for supper."

The coyote whimpered. Terrified, he kicked his feet and struggled to get up. It took hardly any effort at all for me to hold him down. The smell of his fear was so strong that it burned my nose. It almost made my eyes water.

Suddenly I began to wonder why Poky wasn't with us. I looked around. A bit nervous, scared that something bad might have happened to my friend, I was just about to let go of the coyote and search for Poky when another coyote shot through the broken boards on Poky's side of the fence.

"Would you look at him?" I told Red.

The coyote raced across the yard. He whimpered and yapped and squalled every step of the way. And there, behind him, was Poky—still holding on to his hind leg and flopping like a flag waving in the breeze.

The coyote shot through the hole into Red's yard.

"Poky," I called, "let go of that coyote and come over here."

Poky didn't answer. In a moment or two the coyote shot back through the hole under the fence, headed in the other direction. The beagle still clung to his leg as he crawled through the boards into Poky's yard.

"Poky," Red called, "let go of him and come here."

Again there was no answer.

Yapping and screaming and crying, the coyote—with the beagle still hanging on to his leg—raced back and forth between the two holes in the fence about five times.

Finally Red turned to me.

"Reckon I should go get him?"

I shrugged my ears. "Guess so. If you don't,

he'll keep chewing on that poor coyote's leg all night."

The big coyote—the one that I was holding down—tried to slip free. I bopped him on the head with my paw.

"Be still!"

Red trotted to the hole in Poky's fence. This time, as the coyote came slipping through, Red leaned down and caught ahold of Poky's tail.

"Let go of me!" Poky growled. "I'm gonna chew this guy's leg off."

It was a bit hard to understand him because he had a mouthful of coyote leg.

Red didn't let go. He held on to Poky's tail. The coyote stopped. With Poky hanging on to his leg and Red hanging on to Poky, the coyote tried to run, but he couldn't. He kept jerking and struggling to get away.

It reminded me of a tug-of-war game. Red on one side, the coyote on the other. And Poky was the rope. The beagle was stretched out between the two bigger animals. His feet dangled about six inches off the ground.

"Let go, Poky!" Red growled. "He's had enough."

It was a bit hard to understand Red because he had a mouthful of beagle tail.

Finally, Poky released his grip. Still crying, the

coyote limped for the back of the yard. His leg must have really hurt, because it took him three jumps before he finally got over the fence. Then he whimpered and limped off into the darkness.

Red licked Poky right on top of the head. "Good job. You really showed him."

"Yeah, I did."

With his head held high on one end and his tail sticking up high on the other, Poky came prancing across the yard.

All three of us glared down at the large coyote—the one with the big mouth.

"What are we gonna do with this one?" Poky asked.

"I don't know," I answered.

"I think we should eat him." Red winked again.

The big coyote struggled, helpless to get up. "Oh, please, please," he begged. "Don't eat me."

"You ate all our food," Poky growled. "Now we don't have anything to eat for supper. We'll *have* to eat you."

Red tilted his head to the side. He sniffed. "I don't know," he said thoughtfully. "If he tastes half as bad as he smells, he would probably make us sick." He made a snorting sound and wrinkled his nose.

"He's right!" the coyote pleaded. "I *do* stink.

Besides that, I'm tough and stringy. You guys wouldn't like me at all."

I smiled at my friends. "I think Poky is right. Even if this coyote does stink, and even if he is a little tough, let's eat him. I'll hold him down and you guys go ahead. After all, it was your food that he ate."

The big coyote cried and whined and wiggled. "Wait," he begged. "Let's talk this over. Let's be friends."

"Oh," I snarled. "So *now* you want to be friends?"

The big coyote whimpered and cried and squalled. We looked down at him. We couldn't keep from sneering at the coward.

Finally I leaned over and picked him up by the tail. He dangled, limply from my mouth. I was so tall that he didn't even touch the ground when I trotted across the yard.

At the back fence I stopped. I aimed with my left eye. With one jerk of my head, I flung the coyote skyward.

He went sailing high up in the air. His feet churned. His tail spun.

Suddenly I realized that was his rear spinning, not his tail. My eyes crossed as I looked down my snout. His tail still dangled from my mouth.

"Oops," I mumbled. "Musta forgot to let go."

The coyote flew so high into the sky that he almost seemed to touch the silver-white moon. Then he came crashing down.

There was a loud *clank* from the other side of the fence. We moved closer and peeked through the cracks between the boards. The big coyote had landed in a trash can. There was more clanking and rattling as the coyote struggled to get out. The trash can finally tipped over. Covered with lettuce, sour milk, used tissues, and all sorts of stinky, yucky stuff, the big coyote came crawling out.

If he'd had his tail, he would have tucked it under him. As it was, he tucked his bottom and went slinking off into the desert. I knew we'd never see the coyotes, ever again.

Chapter 14

Red was a little sore and stiff for a couple of days. Poky went around coughing and spitting and complaining about how bad coyotes tasted. I couldn't help but notice the little twinkle in his eye each time he griped about it, though.

For the next three weeks life was calm and peaceful. We played together when our masters were at work. At night we either slept together in my big doghouse or enjoyed the peace and quiet of sleeping alone in our own yards.

Then one afternoon I heard a rattling sound at my back gate. The hair bristled in a sharp ridge down my back. My muscles tightened.

I watched.

A man opened the gate and peeked in. He wore a black stocking cap. Without a sound I eased to my feet. I had to lean down to see out of my doghouse because I was so tall that my head almost touched the ceiling. The man shut the gate behind him and started across my yard. Then his eyes fell on my huge house. He must have seen me watching. Suddenly he froze. He didn't move, he didn't tremble, he didn't even breathe.

I eased through the doorway and walked on stiff legs toward him.

As I neared, he held out one hand, offering his knuckles for me to sniff. Although he wore a black cap like the burglar, he was not the same man. His face was different, and his smell was not the same as that of the thief who had come in the night.

"Nice dog." His voice quavered. "Nice dog. Hope you're a good dog."

The smell of fear was strong. It hurt my nose, but at the same time it made me feel big and strong inside. I followed him as he eased his way to the back of my master's house. There he moved a bush aside with the back of his hand and looked down at something.

I watched.

"I'm just reading the electric meter," he assured me, looking down at a glass thing that stuck up from some pipes at the back of the house. "Nice dog. I'm not going to bother anything. Good puppy."

He took a sharp pointed thing from his pocket and scratched on a pad. Then he let go of the bush and moved slowly away.

I watched.

But I didn't follow him. His smell of fear was simply a smell of fear. There was no sneaky taste to it. There was nothing sly or evil about the way he moved. He slipped through the gate at the back of my fence and closed it behind him.

Poky came over that afternoon. He was excited and happy because his master had finally gotten him a new chewy bone. When Red crawled through the hole from his side of the fence, Poky offered to share his chewy bone with us.

He was so proud of his new bone that Red and I just didn't have the heart to get slobbers all over it. We decided to at least let Poky chew the new off his bone before we shared it.

It was early spring when trouble came to visit. It came at night, just as it had before. I lay in my doghouse with my paws folded, resting my chin on them where they draped over the edge of my floor.

There was a sound at the back fence. My ears perked.

I watched.

A black stocking cap appeared at the top of my fence. There was a *clunk* as a man's foot found the bottom rail. He climbed over the fence.

I watched.

The man was dressed in black. His shirt was black, and he wore black pants and black gloves. For a moment he hesitated and looked around.

I watched.

Boldly he walked across the yard, straight to my doghouse.

"Hi, you dumb mutt." He smiled. "You remember me? I remember you. You're the same dog who was here last time I broke into this place."

The smell of fear came from him. It was not the simple smell of fear. This was the same sly, sneaky smell that had come from this man when he stole things from my master's house. It was the same sneaky smell that had come from the coyotes when they stole our food. It was the smell of fear that came when someone did something they knew was wrong and they were afraid they might get caught.

I felt the hair stand on end along my back. I eased to my feet.

"I may look like the same dog," I said. "But I'm not. You'd better get out of my master's yard."

But I guess people just don't understand Dog.

The man walked to the back door and started jiggling the doorknob. I walked right up behind him.

"Figure it's been long enough since I was here last for the folks inside to collect their insurance money and buy all new stuff." The man's voice was as sneaky as his smell.

"I warned you," I growled. "You'd better leave. You'd better not rob my master's house again."

He gave me a funny look when I growled at him, but even with my second warning, I guess he still didn't understand. "Beat it, mutt," he said. "I'm busy. Bet the guy's got a new VCR and TV and new everything." He took a long bar from a black bag that he carried. He pushed it into the side of the door and started to pry it open.

I shrugged my ears. "All right. I tried to warn you."

Red and blue lights flashed. Weird, funny shadows danced across my yard. A tall, lean man in a blue uniform stood beside my master. He scratched his head and looked at me. I smiled back. Then he turned to my master.

"I can't quite figure it out, Mr. Shaffer," the

man said. "Your neighbors called us. They reported hearing screams, like someone was being killed. Before you got home, we checked the premises. There's a mark on your back door, as if someone tried to break in with a crowbar or something. And we found a pant leg from a pair of black slacks hanging on your back fence. But that's all we found."

Mr. Shaffer looked at me and scratched his head. "Officer, may I borrow your flashlight for a moment?"

The policeman handed Mr. Shaffer his light and followed him to my doghouse. My master dropped to one knee and shone his light inside. In the back corner of my house were my trophies—my reminders that I wasn't really a bully if I fought to protect myself or my friends.

"See anything?" The policeman leaned down next to him.

Mr. Shaffer almost laughed. "Not much. Just a coyote tail, a crowbar, and a black stocking cap."

The policeman chuckled as he got to his feet. "Looks like an attempted burglary. Your dog must have run the thief off before he could get into the house. Looks like you got yourself one heck of a watchdog there, Mr. Shaffer."

My master grunted as he got to his feet. He

handed the officer his flashlight, then came over and started patting my head.

"Best watchdog a man could ever want," he bragged. "Sweetie, you're some watchdog."

This time, when my master said the word "watchdog," that was exactly what he meant. I felt so big and proud I could have popped. My tail began to wag. It almost knocked the policeman down. It pounded against the side of my doghouse like someone beating on a bass drum.

"You're some watchdog." My master's words drummed in my ears even louder than my tail drummed against my doghouse. Those were the words I had always wanted to hear more than anything else in the world.

"Watchdog."

The word made my chest fill with pride. My tail wagged harder. Suddenly my whole back end was wagging. Then my middle and even my shoulders wagged. I wasn't wagging my tail—my tail was wagging me. Even my ears began to flop. Finally I was a watchdog.

About the Author

BILL WALLACE has had pets for as long as he can remember. He grew up with all sorts of animals around the house.

"Our dogs and cats always got along," Bill said. "Fact was, I just knew they could communicate and tell what the other was thinking."

But a friend of Bill's had a dog who didn't like cats. When he rode over on his bicycle to play, the dog almost got Mike, a Siamese that Bill really liked.

He used that dog for Butch in the book *Snot Stew*. Butch was really a "bad guy." Then a fan wrote and wanted to know why Bill made dogs the villains and told him how his dogs and cats always got along. It was that letter—and the six dogs and one cat that live on the Wallaces' farm in Oklahoma, combined with Bill and Carol's "granddogs"—that gave him the idea for this story.